D0325875

NO
DOgS
Allowed!

NO DOGS Allowed!

BILL WALLACE

Holiday House / New York

Printed in the United States of America

www.holidayhouse.com

3   5   7   9   10   8   6   4   2

Library of Congress Cataloging-in-Publication Data
Wallace, Bill, 1947–
No Dogs Allowed! / by Bill Wallace.—1st ed.
p. cm.
Summary: Eleven-year-old Kristine, still struggling to come
to terms with the death of her family's beloved horse, finds it difficult
to accept the new dog she receives for her birthday.
ISBN-13: 978-0-8234-1818-3 (hardcover)
ISBN 0-8234-1818-9 (hardcover)

[1. Dogs—Fiction. 2. Grief—Fiction. 3. Pets—Fiction. 4. Death—Fiction.
5. Friendship—Fiction. 6. Family life—Fiction.] I. Title.

PZ7.W15473No 2004
[Fic]—dc22
2003056756

to

Dandy

for the inspiration

Carol

for starting the story, then making me finish it

Regina Griffin

for whittling it down to size

NO
DOGS
Allowed!

chapter 1

The big yellow school bus turned onto the gravel section line road. Bits of rock popped against the bottom of the bus, hitting so hard I could almost feel them through my tennis shoes.

"Kristine, do you think we'll get to play on the A string this year?" Selena asked.

"I don't know. We've been practicing since the first day of school, but we didn't get to play much last year when we were fourth graders."

Some older boys began scuffling with one another. Mrs. Martin, the bus driver, stopped the bus and glanced at her rearview mirror.

"Gentlemen. Settle down so we can go." She looked stern. "I'd like to get home before dark!"

Everyone on the bus turned to look back at the boys, including me.

"What are *you* looking at, Curly Sue?" A sixth-grade boy behind us called.

"I'm looking at hot air." I crinkled my nose before I turned back around.

"How do boys get so annoying?" Selena whispered.

"They get it from their friends." I poked my fingers into my curly ponytail, then straightened my bangs.

"I wish I was still in Texas." Selena frowned.

"But you wouldn't have met me, if you'd stayed in Texas." I jostled her arm.

"You're right. The only thing . . . in Texas, I didn't have to ride the bus with boys. Are you going to join the Y team?"

I shrugged. "Don't know yet. The baby, you know. Everything revolves around that."

"When's your mom supposed to have it?"

I looked out the window. We were almost to Meme C's.

"The baby," Selena said. "When's it due? Is that why you're going to your grandmother's today?"

"Meme says that babies are born when they get good and ready. But she also says that a full moon will be here soon and that makes a difference with livestock." I grinned. "Mama tells Meme that she's having a baby, not a calf."

"Your mom does look pretty big!" Selena teased.

"Whisper. I don't want those boy-goons to get started on that. Mama has two weeks before the baby's supposed to be here. I get to ride the bus to my grandparents, while she's training another girl to take over her job at the bank."

I stood up when the bus stopped.

"Phone me when you get home," Selena called.

"See you tomorrow, Curly Sue," a voice squeaked from behind me.

I didn't look back. I knew it was that bug-brained Matt.

As the bus drove off, I jerked around to look. Sure enough, Matt's face was plastered against the window. He had his eyes crossed, and his tongue stuck out the corner of his mouth. *Boys!* I started stomping up the road to Meme C's.

When the roar of the bus faded in the distance, I leaned my head to the side. The sound should come any second now. The little whinny. It didn't matter if Meme C had fed her or not, Dandy would always call at me—tell me she was starving.

But all I could hear was the crunch of my tennis shoes. I froze in my tracks. My stomach tightened when I remembered. Dandy wouldn't whinny at me today. The gentle old horse wasn't there anymore.

I stared at the old shade tree, near the fallen

log. I could almost see her. Every day the old white horse stood tall in the pasture. Sometimes she came to the fence for a little pat on her head. Other times, she just followed one of her paths up the hill, then came around the back of the house to get her sugar snack. I would talk to her. I'd tell her secrets. I'd scratch behind her ears. She'd close her eyes and . . .

Meme and Papa called to tell us. Mama and I fought the tears back for a while.

In fact, I hadn't really cried until I was alone in my room. For the next two weeks, I kept all thoughts of her out of my head. I was over it. She was Mama's horse, not mine.

Now I felt a tear roll down my cheek when I looked at the old log.

She wasn't there.

chapter 2

I opened the storm door and dumped my school stuff on the chair. "I'm here, Meme."

Meme peeked around the corner from the kitchen.

"Homework today, Kristine?" she asked, wiping her hands on a towel. Eyes twinkling, she planted a quick kiss on my forehead.

"It won't take long. My math is already done and I have one page of social studies to look up. Can I go down to the pasture for a minute or two? Mama has to pick up Anna from day care. That always takes awhile." I wrapped my arms around her waist.

"Just a few minutes or two." Meme hugged me back. "Your dad's picking Anna up today. So don't stay gone too long." Meme pushed my bangs away from my face. "I promised your mother that I'd help you check your homework."

"I won't be long. I'm going right down there." I pointed to a big tree in the pasture.

"The thinking tree?" Meme patted me on the head. "Is that old log still in one piece?"

"Pretty much."

I walked out the door, across the front yard, and crawled through the fence that surrounded the front pasture. The top strand was barbed wire and the two strands below were smooth. Papa called it pony wire. Dandy was just three months old when he put the fence up around the pasture. He said that he didn't want her to get all scratched up.

Before Dandy was born they'd had a quarter horse foal that had run into one of the old five-strand barbed-wire fences and ripped up her whole chest. After a big veterinarian bill she was okay, but it had taken a long time before she healed. Papa said that she named herself, though. Bar-B-Wire. They called her Barbie.

Marching through the tall love grass, I came to one of the paths that Dandy had made as she wandered around the pasture. A knot came up in my throat.

I followed the path to the pecan tree where Dandy and I used to talk and plopped down on the fallen log.

Mama was just six years old when Dandy was

born. Meme said that Great-Papa Wilton was very excited about that little filly. Even though his cows had calves all the time, there was something about the little foal that had made his chest puff up and a big smile tug at his face.

A warm trickle ran from my cheek to my chin. I fought the tears for a moment, then, sure no one was around to see, I let go.

"Take off your shoes at the door, Kristine." Meme stared at the knees of my jeans. "Let's wash your pants. Be one less thing for your mom to worry about. Grab a pair of my old sweats out of that middle drawer. I'll meet you in the washroom."

The washing machine was almost filled when I handed her my jeans.

"Meme, do you miss Dandy?"

"Of course I do." Meme's shoulders tightened, but she kept scrubbing the knees of my jeans. "What makes you ask such a question?"

"I don't know. You just seem to act so . . . normal, I guess."

"Kristine, we had that old horse for twenty-eight years. Your mom was just a little girl when that horse was born. She thought Dandy was all hers."

"I know, Meme. Mama was the *only* one who got to ride her for a long time."

"We all loved that horse. It was a painful decision about letting her go."

"But Dandy's mother lived to be thirty-four. Didn't you think she was going to live longer?"

Meme leaned back against the washer. "Twenty-eight is old for a horse. The horse I grew up with died when he was only sixteen. Twenty-eight years is a *long* time."

"But it's so sad. I can see her standing by the fence, waiting for me." I swallowed hard.

Meme's smile was soft. "I know, Kristine. There's a place where the yard light kind of shines over by the edge of the barn. She always stood there. I looked out the other night and I could almost see her ears perk up."

I fought back a tear. "I really didn't ride her very much. I just expected her to be here forever."

Meme patted my hand. "We did everything we could. It was just her time to go."

"Maybe it would be better if we just didn't have pets," I said, pulling my hand away.

Meme frowned. "Let's talk about something else. You want a snack? How was school today?"

"School's still there," I answered, following her toward the kitchen.

"Anything exciting happen?"

"No."

"What did you do in gym class?"

"Nothing."

"How about the ride home on the bus?"

"That stupid Matt keeps pestering me. I wasn't bothering him. For no reason, he starts calling me Curly Sue."

"Matt Green?"

"Yeah. He's in the sixth grade."

"When he was little," Meme said, smiling over her shoulder, "he had the curliest hair you've ever seen. What does his hair look like now?"

"He's bald with green horns coming out of the top of his head."

"Then he's really changed. I think I have a picture of him." She went to the cabinet in the living room, where she kept all of her picture albums and scrapbooks.

"You'll never find it. Besides, Matt was always ugly. Let's eat."

Meme thumbed through piles of pictures. "Here it is." She trotted back to me. "Look at what a sweetie he was."

I stared at the sweet little baby face, then shook my head. "No, that's not him. Matt Green was born with horns."

"Look at his eyes. Eyes don't change much. That has to be the same kid."

"Okay. You win. He must keep his hair really short now so his horns show up better."

Meme smiled. "Either that or maybe he's hiding *his* curly hair."

"Why does he have to be such a jerk?"

Meme gave me a little grin. "Maybe he was just trying to get you to notice him."

My cheeks suddenly felt *really* warm. "After school snack? Homework to check, remember?"

Meme found a small bag of chips and fixed me a sandwich. Social studies was no problem. Meme checked it when I was done. Then she got my math paper. Math was *not* one of my favorite subjects. Five out of ten problems were wrong. Homework would have been easier if Meme C just told me the answers, but instead she dragged me through each problem, making me think. At least it kept my mind off Dandy.

I was about halfway through the last problem when I heard Papa's old tractor. The door squeaked open, and he strolled in and gave Meme a big hug.

"I sure do miss that old horse," he said.

Papa reached out and ruffled my hair. "Hi, Squirt!"

Meme noticed the look on my face. "Thinking about Dandy again?"

I nodded but couldn't answer her.

chapter 3

We stood together with our arms around one another for a few minutes. I tried to feel every detail—the way Meme smelled of flour and baked bread; the odor of fresh dirt on Papa's bib overalls; the tenderness of their hugs—I tried to pull all that into my head and keep it there forever.

Meme let go and scurried toward the laundry room. "Gotta get those jeans in the dryer. Lauren will be here soon and Kristine will have to wear wet pants home."

"Weren't you making cookies today?" Papa called after her.

"Stay out of my cookie dough!" Meme scolded. "Remember what your doctor said. I'm watching you."

Papa gave a little snort and winked at me.

"No, she's not. Come on."

There was no cookie dough on the stove. We looked on the counter, in the oven, and even in the refrigerator again. Papa stood in the center of the kitchen. Frowning, he took his cap off, held it by the bill, and scratched his head.

"I tell you . . . that woman's got a sixth sense when it comes to protecting her cookie dough."

Suddenly Papa's eyes darted in my direction.

"The dishwasher? She'd never hide cookie dough in there, Papa."

He wiggled his eyebrows up and down. "Never?"

"I don't think so."

"Let's see." He reached for the door latch and pulled it open. "That's funny. Sure looks a lot like her mixing bowl."

"Must be a bowl that she used the last time she fixed cookies." I handed Papa a clean spoon.

"Don't dig out of the same spot each time," Papa whispered. "Spread it around so she won't know we've been into it."

"You two, stop! You're gonna make yourselves sick." Meme shouldered her way between us, grabbed her own spoon, and joined in.

"I've been eating cookie dough for over fifty years and I never got sick. Not even once."

"How about the time, when we were first married, and you ate the whole pan?"

Papa stuck his tongue out at her. "Okay . . . maybe one time. But that was your fault. You doubled the recipe."

Meme winked at me, then kissed him on the cheek. We ate for a while, savoring each spoonful. I loved chocolate chip cookies, but there was something about getting into the dough . . . somehow, it tasted twice as good.

"Better eat a couple of these cookies, Lauren," Meme called when Mama came in the front door. "Your dad and daughter get into the dough again, you won't even get a taste."

"Kristine, have you been into the dough?" Mama gave me a quick hug. Her round tummy kept me from getting too close.

"Papa made me do it."

"Hope you didn't eat too much," Mama said. "Soon as your dad calls, we need to take off and meet him and Anna at Eduardo's. That is, unless you want to save Eduardo's until next week for your birthday. What do you think?"

Birthday? I hadn't even thought about my birthday coming up. Everything at home was baby, baby, baby.

"Eduardo's is fine." I grinned. "I could eat *queso* and chips every day of the week."

"Chips, cheese, and salsa will be your dessert, *after* you've eaten." Mama's face grimaced as she climbed onto the stool. "Thanks for watching Kristine. This overtime is wearing me out."

Meme nodded, but before she could say, "you're welcome," the phone rang. Mama picked it up. Meme snapped her fingers and pointed to the washroom.

I tugged my jeans on. My shirt was the nicest one I had, so I dug around in Meme's drawer, looking for one of hers. I found the perfect one. It already had a stain on it.

"Come on, Kristine. We've got to go."

"Later, 'gator," Meme called to us as we hurried for the car.

chapter 4

"Hurry, Kristine. Your dad's probably in a huff, waiting for us."

The sun reflected against the wall of the tin barn. For just a second, the old horse popped into my head. I could almost see her ears flick as she watched us leave.

We backed out of the driveway. When we started forward, Mama glanced at me. "Hard day?"

"Kind of. Things were okay, until I got here and started thinking about Dandy. Don't you miss her?"

"Of course I do. She was my best friend for a long time. That old horse heard so many of my secrets . . . well, I was lucky that she couldn't talk!"

"I thought we were going to Eduardo's?" I said, suddenly realizing that we were headed the wrong way.

"I've got to pick up something at the house. It shouldn't take long. You might want to get a better shirt—the one you have on is pretty ratty looking."

"It's perfect! It already has a stain, right here." I outlined the big spot in the middle with my finger.

"You can find one that's a little better looking. Then again, Anna's just as messy at three as you were. She'll probably get you if you look too good."

As soon as I got to my room, I dug through my closet looking for the "perfect" shirt. Not too new, but not too *comfortable*. Meme's T-shirt had that big stain. But if I turned it around, no one would see a stain on the back of it. That way, if Anna was wild, I still didn't have to worry about stains on a clean top.

When I looked out the door, Mama was stuffing something into the back of the car. "Lock up, Kristine," she called, slamming the trunk. "We gotta go!"

There were only ten cars in Eduardo's parking lot.

"Looks like we beat the crowd." I smiled.

Mama nodded. "That's what your dad wanted. No crowd." She parked close to Dad's truck. "Better hurry, he's probably wrestling Anna for the chips."

"If I have to eat my dinner before I get chips, so does Anna." I pouted.

Mama ignored me. When we stepped into the entrance, a tall man smiled and came toward us.

"Hi, Lauren," he greeted.

"Hi, Ed. Is Richard already here?"

He motioned over his shoulder. "We put him in the back room. Come on, I'll show you."

"Why are we in the back room?" I asked Mama as we walked through the restaurant. "They only use that on weekends or when there's a big crowd."

Mama ignored me again.

When we reached the swinging doors, Mama nudged me ahead of her just as Ed opened them. My eyes popped wide. Streamers hung from the ceiling. Clumps of bright balloons waved above some of the chairs. I blinked a couple of times. On the far side of the room a big banner read:

HAPPY BIRTHDAY, KRISTINE!

I blinked again, trying to take it all in. A long table was decorated with paper flowers and presents. At another table were people. *My* people. I looked up at Mama. "This isn't my birthday. Did you forget when I was born?"

Mama let out a little laugh. "Silly. This is a *surprise* party. Are you surprised?"

Before I had a chance to answer, Selena grabbed my arm and dragged me toward the table. "Sit here by me!"

Meme C and Papa sat across from us. Selena's parents were there, too. Daddy was at the end of the table. He glanced up and shot me a quick wink, then went back to wrangling Anna. My other grandparents, Grandma and Grandpa Rankin, were next to them, trying to help. All three were busy scooting things out of Anna's reach, handing her tortilla chips to munch on, or just grabbing for her water glass before she turned it over.

It took all of them to keep Anna from making a total wreck out of that end of the table.

"Happy birthday," Selena whispered.

I gave her a big hug. Then I ran around the table and hugged everyone there.

Mama sat down between Daddy and me. She reached over and gave my hand a squeeze. "We'll have a kid party for you after the baby gets here. We just wanted you to know that we hadn't forgotten you."

"Did you know about this all along?" I turned to Selena.

"Well, sort of." She gave a sheepish grin. "Mother didn't exactly tell me the whole thing. She thought I would give it away. But I didn't, did I?"

"You're a great secret keeper!"

Papa shoved his chair back and stood up. "Speech time," he announced. There was a loud *clank* when his chair tipped and fell to the floor. "Now that I have everyone's attention, I want to congratulate Kristine for getting to be part of this wonderful family. If she hadn't been born . . ."—Papa stretched out his arm and looked at his watch—". . . ten years, three hundred fifty-eight days, and two hours ago, she would have missed a great party."

Everyone clapped.

"Your turn, Kristine. Speech back!" Papa stretched out both arms and bowed to me.

My mind was a total blank. I opened my mouth, but nothing came out.

Under the table, Mama nudged my leg with her knee. "Just say 'thanks,'" she whispered.

My cheeks felt really warm as I slowly stood up. "I—uh—I want to say something. Oh, yeah. I've got it. *Thanks!*"

The waiters had already brought everyone's food to the table. My favorite quesadilla was in front of me.

"Your dad ordered for you," Selena whispered.

The meal was wonderful. When we were through, it was time to open presents. Selena gave me a diary. Grandma and Grandpa Rankin gave me a new billfold with money inside. Selena's mom and dad gave me a bright yellow blouse. When I opened the package and pulled it up for people to see, Selena's mom announced: "Selena said that since Kristine's favorite pastime was dropping cheese on her shirts, we should get yellow, to go well with it."

Everyone laughed.

Mama presented me with a really big box. I'd just taken it from her when her smile disappeared. She winced and kind of tilted to one side.

"Are you okay?" I whispered.

"I'm fine, hon."

But as soon as she said it, little beads of sweat popped out on her forehead. She stood there a moment. "I'm better now," she assured me.

Still trying to keep one eye on Mama, I pulled at the ribbon. Why be neat and tidy opening a birthday present? So I tore into the package, tossing ribbon and paper everywhere. When I finally got the cardboard lid open, all I found was a big chunk of Styrofoam. Mama tilted the box toward me.

"I'll hold. You pull."

"It's a stereo!" I yelped. "The one from the catalog!"

Mama dabbed her forehead with a napkin. "I

don't know what made us get it for you. Maybe it was all the *hints* somebody left lying around the house."

"The speakers are in our closet at home," Daddy called.

I wanted to squeeze Mama as hard as I could but I had to be careful. As soon as I finished hugging her, I raced to Daddy. Daddy *wasn't* pregnant. I hugged him so hard, his eyes almost bugged out of his head.

"Thank you! Thank you! Thank you! . . ."

"It's cake time," Papa said. "Kristine, why don't you come help us carry the cake? It's in the truck."

Papa had a funny grin on his dark wrinkled face. Meme C looked kind of weird, too, when she got up to join us.

"How big *is* this cake?" I asked.

Instead of going out the front of the restaurant, Papa led the way through the kitchen.

"You parked out back?"

He didn't answer. He simply walked through the back door and held it until Meme C and I came through. His truck was just outside. Papa took my left hand in his left hand. Then he spun around and reached back with his right hand. I took it, too.

"Left, right, left, right," he called over his shoulder.

"Close your eyes."

I was dying to see what the surprise was.

"No peeking! Stay put!"

The tailgate dropped down.

"Now, Papa?" I could hear my voice quiver.

"Not yet."

There was another sound. Papa was dragging something across the bed of the truck. Then a faint scratching, scraping sound. And then . . .

"Yip, yip."

My heart sank clear down into the bottom of my tennis shoes.

"Yip, yip," the bark came again.

"Okay, Kristine." Papa's voice was almost a laugh. "You can turn around now."

Only, I couldn't turn around. Not now.

"Look, Kristine. She's all yours." Papa's voice was excited and proud.

"I don't want a puppy!" I blurted out as I whirled around to face him.

My papa couldn't have looked more surprised or hurt if I had doubled up my fist and slugged him in the stomach.

"You—you don't want the puppy?" he stammered.

"I—I—well, I—er—" All I could do was stammer.

A puppy was the last thing in the world I wanted. But when I said I didn't want a puppy, it hurt Papa. I didn't want to hurt him any more than I already had.

"I—ah—" I stammered again. "What I meant to say, Papa, was that I don't want a puppy—right now. We can't take it into the restaurant."

"Oh, sure we can," he said. "I already cleared it with Ed—that's why we're in the back. We have to wrap her in a coat or something, when we go back in. But he said it's fine. I promised Ed that I'd mop up personally if she had an accident."

With that, he shoved the puppy into my arms.

I took her. There was nothing else I could do.

chapter 5

"Come on, you two," Meme said. She stood beside the cab of the truck with a flat box in her arms. "This cake is getting heavy."

The yellow puppy squirmed and wiggled in my arms, trying to lick my face. I didn't look at her, but I did look at Meme. Her eyes cut right into me.

Meme always knew when I was lying.

Papa threw a sweater around the dog to cover it from view. Papa and I were both glowing—he with pride, me from embarrassment.

As soon as we walked into the party, Selena raced to us.

"Can I hold her?" she squealed. "She's so cute. Can I hold her?"

I shoved the dog into her arms and went back to my chair.

"Come on, Kristine. These candles are melting," Papa said, tugging me closer to the cake.

"Okay, everybody. On three. One, two —"

When Papa got to "three" I blew the candles out. While they sang "Happy Birthday," Meme C and Grandma Rankin served the cake and ice cream. Just as Selena started to take her second bite, the little pup's tongue flicked out at the ice cream. Selena giggled.

The muscles in my face tightened as I fought back a smile.

I'd only taken a few bites when I felt hands on my shoulders.

"Kristine. We've got to go."

I jerked my head around. Daddy leaned over, right beside my ear.

"What?"

"It's the baby. We're going to have to get your mother to the hospital."

Mama stood by the door, bent over just a bit. I started to run to her, but she waved at me to sit back down.

"It's okay, Kristine," Daddy whispered. "Stay here and finish your party. As soon as everything is over, Meme and Papa will bring you to the hospital. Grandma and Grandpa Rankin will bring Anna. You won't miss anything important. I promise."

"I want to go with you. Please."

"You'll be there before the baby comes. We have plenty of time." Daddy patted my head, then gave me a hug.

"Love you, Kristine." Mama smiled. "Finish your party. Meme will bring you to the hospital."

It took *forever* to get our things together. At least it felt like it did. The drive to the hospital took even longer. I had to hold the puppy. She was all over the place, trying to look out the window, chewing on my thumb, and licking my face. When we finally got there, Papa put the pup into the little cage in the back of the truck and we hurried inside.

Mama's room was pretty ordinary. She was propped up in bed with a white sheet over her. I held her hand.

"Is this where I was born?" I asked.

"Well, sort of. They've remodeled since you and Anna came." Mama suddenly let go of my hand and gripped the side of her bed.

"Does it hurt?" I stared at her.

"It's worth it to get this baby born."

Papa kissed Mama's forehead. "We better go check on your pup, Kristine. Your mother has some work to do."

Daddy said, "I'll let you know as soon as anything happens."

I followed Papa into the waiting area. Meme C was reading to Anna in the corner, and Selena and her mother stood looking at a bulletin board on the wall.

"Come look at these babies!" Selena called to me. "This kid has more hair than Korey, and he's only one day old."

"Hey, girls, let's go check on the pup. She won't be happy if we leave her in that cage all evening," Papa said.

Selena's mom smiled at us. "We can't stay too much longer. But maybe Selena can help make time pass a little faster. Go on, hon."

No sound came from the pet carrier in the back of Papa's pickup. He dropped the tailgate so that we had a place to sit.

"Can we take her out?" Selena asked.

The instant the puppy heard a voice, the box wasn't quiet anymore. She was so excited, I thought she was going to tear the thing apart.

"Sure." Papa grinned. "She probably needs to take care of business."

Selena started to reach in, but she never got the chance. The pup came flying from the box, her tail wagging hard and fast, her whole body squirming all over. She raced for the edge of the tailgate, but

27

realizing how high up she was, locked her little legs. The metal pickup bed was slick under her claws, so if I hadn't grabbed her at the last second, she would have fallen—flat on her little puppy nose.

"She's so cute." Selena giggled. "Isn't she the most adorable thing you ever saw?"

The pup did look pretty cute. Innocent. Sweet.

Papa dug around in the cab of the pickup, then pulled out a little bag. "Mealtime! Kristine, take her over to that grassy area, then we'll give her a little grub."

I offered the pup to Selena. "Here you go."

Papa had a funny look on his face. "She's your pup, Kristine. You need to be responsible."

Tucking her under my arm like a football, I stomped toward the grassy spot under the light pole.

The pup's sharp little claws scratched my arm. Her baby teeth chewed my fingers. Her bright eyes looked up at me.

"She's so cute," Selena's voice oozed like sap dripping from a tree. "I wish we could get a puppy."

"Wish you could have this one," I grumbled.

"No dogs for us." Selena sighed. "My stepsister is allergic to pet dander. When she comes to visit we have to have the house *immaculate*. I think she's faking—her house isn't that clean. But when she visits *us,* we're on dust alert."

28

"She looks pretty healthy to me." I dropped the pup on the grass.

"I guess," Selena agreed. "Her big problem is her age. Sixteen. She thinks she's a grown-up, which makes me a baby." Selena stuck her thumb in her mouth. "Waaah!"

"Sisters can be a pain. But I really love Anna, and I'm getting ready to have another one." A knot suddenly gripped my stomach as I thought about Mama.

Sharp claws brought me back to where I was and what I was doing. The puppy looked up at me, then backed away a bit. Crouched low to the ground, she wagged her tail. Well, not her tail. Her whole back end wagged. All at once, she sprang and hit my leg again.

"Food's ready, Kristine," Papa called. "When she finishes we'll put her back in the carrier. Then go inside and check on your mom."

"Okay," I said.

The silly pup didn't even bother to sniff her food—she just dug right into it. She acted like she hadn't eaten in weeks.

"Just think, a little baby at your house. I love babies!" Selena gave me a hug.

"I'm kind of scared," I heard myself whisper.

"Oh, Kristine." Selena laughed. "Babies are born every day."

"Not *our* baby."

"They are watching your mom carefully. They know what to do."

I looked up at Mama's window. "I'm still scared. I don't want anything to happen to Mama or the baby. Look what happened to Dandy."

"Dandy? Wasn't she about thirty years old?" Selena tilted her head to the side.

"How old do you think Mama is?"

"I don't know."

"Thirty-four!" I snapped before she could even guess.

"That's in people-years, silly. Horse-years are different. Dog-years are about seven, for every one of ours. I don't know what horse-years are."

"Mama was twenty-three when I was born. Thirty-one when Anna came. She's old now."

"Kristine! My mom was forty when I was born. Do you think she's old?"

"No, but she's not having a kid, either."

"She could, though," Selena argued. "She knows this one lady who didn't have her first one until she was forty-five. Now they have three! Your mom's going to be fine. Quit worrying!"

There was a puppy lying across my lap. Without even thinking, I picked her up in my arms and snuggled her. The instant I did, she started licking my face.

She chased the worry and fear away. It's really hard to worry about something when you're getting your face washed with a long, floppy tongue.

Suddenly Papa nudged me with his elbow. "Think something's going on," he said, pointing toward the hospital.

Meme C stood in front, looking around for us. When she spotted Papa, she waved, motioning for us to come.

I put the puppy back into the pet carrier and slammed the door. She stuck her nose through the bars and looked up at me with those big brown eyes. She looked sweet—and cute and lovable and . . .

NO! I screamed inside my head. *I'm not going to fall for that.*

chapter 6

My head swayed with the gentle movement. Now and then my chin brushed against my chest—I had never felt so relaxed and comfortable.

We stopped. The stillness was almost as peaceful as the gentle swaying, and . . .

Someone slid into the bus seat next to me and bounced a couple of times.

"What happened? When did the baby finally get here?" Selena's voice screeched in my ear. "What did you name her? It *was* a her, wasn't it?"

Forcing my eyes open, I yawned and held up a finger. "Give me a minute. I didn't get into bed until after three this morning. I'm pretty groggy."

"I figured that you wouldn't even try to go to school today." Selena talked so fast, I could hardly understand her. "Come on. Tell me about the baby. Tell me. Tell me. Tell me."

I glared at her.

"Well? Are you going to tell me about the baby or not? What's her name? Did you name the puppy yet? Come on. Tell me!"

"Sure. *If* it'll shut you up."

Selena shot me a sneer.

"Baby Kate came at 12:07 in the morning. She weighed six pounds and thirteen ounces. When I first saw her, she looked kind of yucky. She cleaned up pretty good, though." I felt my mouth curl to a smile. "She *is* cute!"

"I just love babies!" Selena's gushy voice seemed to screech in my ear. "You're going to have so much fun. A new baby *and* a new puppy. When do they get to go home?"

"Probably tomorrow. Since she was *actually* born today, I think they will have Mama stay another night."

"Okay, so the baby is Kate. What did you name the puppy?" Selena leaned her knees toward me.

"The puppy? Oh, yeah, the puppy. She could be Whiny or Annoying. I was so tired when we finally got to Meme C's, I went straight to bed. Meme said they let her sleep with them. Maybe Spoiled would be a good name for that mutt."

"You are soooo lucky, Kristine. I've wanted a

puppy for a long time. But now, I guess I'll just have to come visit you more often."

"Hey, Curly Sue, you get a new dog?" Matt propped his chin on the back of our seat. The two second graders he'd shoved over when he sat down were practically on top of each other.

"Did ya get a new dog, Curly Sue?" Matt repeated.

"Back off, birdbrain. Kristine's in no mood to put up with you."

"Who put you in charge, cat-box breath?" He leaned back toward me. "I just wanted to know about your new dog. What kind is it?" Matt's eyes twinkled. "Is it a hunting dog or a—"

"The dog is a stinky fur ball—just like you," I snapped.

The twinkle left Matt's eyes.

"Forget you, Curly Sue."

"Guess what?" Selena blurted out when we reached our locker section.

"What?" Kayla Howard leaned back so she could see around her locker door. Leah looked up, too.

"Kristine's mom had her baby last night."

Almost instantly we were surrounded. It seemed like every girl on our end of the hall came rushing up. The questions flew from all sides.

"Her name is Kate," I announced. "It's kind of a nickname for my grandmother. Her name is Catherine. So Kate . . . nickname . . . sort of. Anyway, she weighs six pounds and thirteen ounces. Her hair is kind of . . . kind of . . . well, she really doesn't have very much hair. I guess it's blondish. Sort of like mine."

During PE I got to tell my story again, since the sixth-grade girls hadn't heard about it yet. Selena also made sure that they knew I had a puppy.

We played softball. Even though our team lost, it was still fun.

The rest of the day was okay, too. When we went to lunch, there were a bunch of pictures posted on the wall where we lined up to get our trays. The photos were of twelve pair of legs! Some of them hairy. Some with knobby knees. Some smooth and glamorous. Everyone looked and laughed and pointed as we waited in line. Mrs. Apple, the counselor, waited until everyone had their trays and sat down. She called for us to get quiet and told us that next Tuesday, during an assembly, we were going to have a Legs Contest. All we had to do was match the pictures of the legs to the teachers they belonged to.

On the way outside for recess, we all stopped again for a closer look. Since there were only three men in the building, it was kind of easy. Mr. Wheat, the principal, had to be the one with the flip-flops. Mr. James, the custodian, was the one with the bowlegs. He sometimes wore shorts to school, so his were easy. Mr. Arrington, the fourth-grade teacher, was kind of hard. He had a mustache and really hairy arms. The legs with the fuzzy slippers were probably his, but they weren't really as hairy as they should be.

All the others were pretty confusing. Each class had a copy of the photos to look at in their classroom. The original pictures were to stay in the cafeteria.

Tired and sleepy as I was, I somehow managed to stay awake all day. When the bell finally rang, I could hardly wait to get to Meme C's and take a short nap.

"Hey, Curly Sue. Wait up!" Matt yelled at me from the doorway.

"Don't call me that!" I kept walking toward the bus.

"Kristine, can I get off at your stop and see your new dog?" I ignored him.

"Kristine? Can I?"

My cheeks felt hot.

"I want to see your new puppy. I really love dogs."

"No," I snapped. "My papa wouldn't like that very much."

Matt shot me a puzzled look. "I know your grandpa. He wouldn't care. He's really nice."

My cheeks felt warm and my ears tingled when I slipped into the first empty seat. Matt stopped—right beside my seat—and looked down at me.

"Please?"

"No. Not today."

Selena plopped down.

"Did Matt go?" I whispered.

"Matt? Matt Green?" Selena twisted in the seat to look. "Yeah. He's back four rows. Why?"

"No reason," I lied.

"Yes. Reason," she urged. "What did he do?"

I slid down in the seat, trying to make myself invisible.

When I peeked back, the eighth-grade boy next to Matt, had a big smile on his face. He poked Matt in the ribs with his finger. "There's your little girlfriend, Matt."

"She's not my girlfriend." Matt shoved the other boy back.

"Is too. I saw you talking to her."

It seemed like the longest bus ride of my life. I was so hot and it felt like I was going to pop. I could see the headlines now:

GIRL EXPLODES ON BUS. SEE PAGE 6 FOR DETAILS.

I wanted to be invisible.

Only two more stops and I could get off. But there was Matt. What if *he* got off at Meme's, too?

"Selena!" I yelled so loud that it startled me as much as it did her. I forced my voice to a whisper. "Go sit by Matt. Make sure he doesn't follow me home."

Selena's nose crinkled. "Yuck. Are you crazy? Why do you think he's going to follow you home?"

"Matt said he wanted to come see the puppy. I'll die if he follows me."

"Tell you what. If he tries to get off, I'll trip him flat to the ground." Selena stuck her left foot out into the aisle and wobbled it around.

"You promise?"

"I promise. But he won't follow you. Without a note from home, saying he has permission to get off at a different stop, Mrs. Martin would have a fit."

We slowed at Meme's driveway. As I pulled myself out of the seat and headed for the door, I saw a movement behind me.

chapter 7

I eased my way to the door before the bus came to a complete stop. Mrs. Martin shot me a look, but she didn't say anything. As soon as the bus doors swung open, I jumped the steps and took off. If Matt was going to follow *me* home, he'd have to run.

I was already halfway up the drive when the bus pulled away. Thank goodness, no Matt. Then, for some weird reason, I felt a little sad. For the life of me, I didn't know why.

When I got to the front porch, the smell of warm cookies tweaked my nose.

"Hey, Meme. Got milk?"

Nobody answered except the puppy, who started yapping. I ignored her. Cookies were in three stages—raw cookie dough in the pan, cookies in the oven, and more on the cooling rack.

"Meme?" I shouted a little louder. "Where are you?"

"Kristine? Is that you?" Meme's voice sounded as though it were coming from inside a box. "I'm working on the bedroom closet."

The timer started buzzing. "Your cookies are done."

"Would you get them?"

"Sure. I'll start the next batch, if you want me to." Before I got to the kitchen, the pup began hitting the door with her front paws.

"Quit that!" I scolded.

Her ears perked, but she didn't leave the door.

"I mean it!"

Tail wagging, she propped her front paws back on the screen again. Ignoring her, I marched to the counter, got the next sheet ready, and started a new batch. Just as I sneaked a quick dip with my fingers, Meme walked in.

"I thought it was just Papa who got into my cookie dough," Meme said, trying to sound stern.

"He just handed this to me!"

"Funny." Meme pretended to look all around. "I'm pretty sure that he's not even here this afternoon."

"Somebody talking about me?"

While Papa slipped through the back door, the pup darted in, but Papa managed to catch her with his foot and get her back outside. "Have you told this puppy hello?"

"Sure did," I lied.

"She's been really good today." Meme finished putting the dough on the cookie sheet.

"Have you decided on a name yet?" Papa reached around Meme for a fingerful of cookie dough. "I like Lola."

"*Lola?*" Meme pretended to swat Papa's hand. "Where did you come up with that?"

"Yeah, Papa. Lola's a weird name for a dog."

He raised his hands over his head and snapped his fingers. Suddenly he spun around and started wiggling—like he was dancing or something.

"What's with Disco Danny?" Meme asked.

"I don't know. He's scaring me!" I pretended to hide behind her.

Papa hummed a chorus of an old song, "Copacabana." He snapped his fingers and wiggled for a moment, then grabbed me and spun me. We danced around the kitchen. Well, we really weren't dancing—Papa was kind of dragging me.

"Get ready!" Papa whispered. "I'm going to dip you!"

Papa took both my hands in his right, then we stepped together, almost touching. He murmured: "Now." I fell backward and kicked my right foot into the air.

An instant before my head hit the floor, Papa stopped my fall. Then he slowly set me down, flat on my back.

"Hey, that's not how it ends. You're supposed to pull me back up."

Before I could get up, Papa was in the cookie dough! When it came to cookies, I was in second place.

"So how was school today, Kristine?"

I wanted to ask Papa if he really knew Matt. I struggled to think of something else to tell him.

"We played softball and I got to be one of the captains."

"Was it fun?"

"Yeah, but we lost, 5 to 1."

"But did you have fun?"

I smiled and nodded.

Papa smiled back, then he turned his attention toward the yapping mutt at the back door. "Now get that poor little abused dog. She needs some attention and exercise."

I trotted over. When I opened the door, her tail wagged so hard that her whole rear end jerked back and forth. A laugh almost slipped out, but I caught myself.

Don't laugh at her. Don't love her. I looked toward the spot where Dandy always stood.

"Well?" Papa called.

When I finally opened the door wider, the goofy thing tripped over her own big paws, slid on her chin, then ran around in a big circle, leaving a wet trail behind her.

"Meme," I squeaked. "I need something to clean this up."

"She's so happy to see you." Papa laughed. "Pick her up and I'll wipe the floor."

"She leaks!" I complained. Finally catching her, I held her at arm's length.

"Take her outside and let her romp. She's just excited. After she's had some playtime she'll be fine inside," Papa said as he grabbed some paper towels.

"We're going to the pasture." I opened the door.

"We're leaving for the hospital in a little bit, so stay close enough so you can hear me call. And don't lose the pup, okay?"

"Okay." I glared down at the little dog. "Come on, dog."

She bounded after me.

As soon as I opened the gate, she took off, but she didn't go very far.

She couldn't follow when I squeezed between the wire on the pasture fence. I picked her up, lifted her through, and plopped her in the tall grass. She just sat and looked at me.

So I went back, picked her up, and carried her to the tree. When I set her down, she suddenly came to life. She sniffed and sniffed the log, her nose wiggling as she smelled all around. I stretched out on the thinking log, shaded by the branches. I closed my eyes, thinking about Mama and Anna and the new baby.

Then somehow, I was imagining Matt Green smiling at me. That made me mad—I didn't want *him* in my head. How long I lay there, I don't know. I was almost asleep when I heard a whinny sound.

I sat straight up, almost losing my balance, but somehow caught myself before I fell off the log. My eyes searched for Dandy's spot by the pecan tree.

Nothing.

A knot tightened in my stomach. The sound came again.

This time I recognized it—it wasn't a whinny after all, it was my name.

"Kristine," Meme called again.

"Coming, Meme."

I'd only taken a couple of steps when I remembered the dumb dog. It would be a lot quicker carrying her to the house than trying to get her to follow me.

Another knot rippled through my stomach, only this time it was worse. I could hardly breathe.

The dog . . . she was gone!

chapter 8

My chest felt like a load of bricks was piled on it. How could I lose her? Only a second ago she was sniffing around not more than six feet away from me.

"Here, dog. I see you," I lied. "Come on. Right now!"

No dog.

Don't panic! I told myself. *She's here someplace.*

She couldn't have gotten very far away. I scanned the pasture.

"Come on, Rover. Dixie. Pumpkin. Lassie," I called. "Bark! Answer me! Say something!"

I hadn't had that dog a whole day and I'd already lost her. I didn't want another pet, but I *sure* didn't want to explain to Papa that I lost his birthday present.

"Kristine. Time to go," Meme called again.

"Just a minute. We're on our way." My heart thumped in my throat.

"Come here, dog." I whispered. I had to find that pup. If only I hadn't been thinking about stupid Matt Green . . .

"Matt. Matt. Matt!" I growled.

Suddenly, the pup shot from a pile of tall grass straight for me. As soon as she bounced her front paws against my leg, I swooped her up in my arms.

"Where have you been? You gave me a scare." I glared at her. "We better get back to the house."

I carried the pup through the pasture to the house.

"We're here," I called.

"Wash up. We're going to the hospital in ten minutes."

"What do you want to do with Matt?" I asked.

"What mat?" Meme peeked around the doorway.

"The dog. Matt." I lifted her toward Meme.

"Kristine. You named the dog Matt? She's a girl. Couldn't you come up with a girl's name?"

"She named herself." I shrugged. "She comes to the name Matt."

"How about Mattie, Madaline, or Madison?" Meme urged.

"Okay. Mattie. But I'll call her Matt."

Meme just shook her head.

"Put her out in the backyard. She'll be fine."

Papa brought daisies for Mama's room. Meme took cookies for the nurses. I got to hold Kate.

Kate's little scrunched-up face twitched, just a bit, as she lay quietly. Her button nose flared when she breathed in and out. Her tiny ears lay flat against her head. Bits of curly hair spiraled on the top. My finger looked huge as I wiggled it into Kate's grasp. She seemed to hold it for a little hug. I felt happy all over.

It was almost dark when we got to Meme and Papa's house. The puppy was yapping in the backyard. By the time we got out of the car, she was jumping at the fence so hard, it sounded like she was going to break through the chain link.

"Kristine, go play with the pup for a little bit." Papa smiled. "She missed you."

"Can't. I have homework."

The corners of Papa's mouth always curled up when he talked about the pup. Now his lips curved down.

"You usually don't have homework on the weekend."

"Social studies test next week. I have to reread

some stuff, and I have a book report due next Friday. I haven't read the book, yet."

Papa sighed. "Get your work done, then. I'll play with her."

I pulled my social studies book out of my backpack. The test wasn't until Wednesday, but I did have to review some. I could hear Papa talking to the little dog in the backyard. She jumped up and he shoved her down. Each time, he laughed when she spun in a circle and raced right back to him.

For an instant, I almost smiled.

Instead, I took my book to the couch, tucked up in a ball, and pretended to study until it was time for bed.

Morning sunshine spread across the bottom of the futon. Something wiggled against my left side. I opened a sleepy eye to see what it was—the dog's head was tucked under my arm, while the rest of her was curled up, tight against my side.

As soon as I raised my head, her tail started to wag. Her little whiskers tickled my face and a wet tongue slopped across my cheek and the corner of my mouth. I pushed her away, but she just hopped right back and tried to lick me again. When she wouldn't quit, I wrapped my arm around her and shoved her down on the bed. Almost immediately she closed her eyes and got really still. I tried to get in a few more minutes of sleep.

When I relaxed my hold on her, the pup stood up, walked around in a circle, and *threw* herself back down on the bed. I peeked out of one eye and couldn't help but smile. She was sound asleep, but her whiskers twitched, and her front feet wiggled as if she were chasing something in a dream. I touched her softly to calm her. She groaned, then stretched her front paws.

"Kristine. Are you awake?" Meme whispered from the doorway.

"Just barely. How did this dog get in here?" Trying *not* to disturb the pup, I pushed the covers back and sat up, ever so slowly.

It didn't work. The instant I moved, she was wide awake, trying to lick my face.

"Papa did it. She kept whining at your door, so he finally let her in."

Papa appeared behind Meme at the open doorway. "Darndest thing I ever saw." He laughed. "She just melted up against you and fell sound asleep." He shook his head. "What did you do?"

"I didn't even know she was in here." I yawned. "Not until I woke up."

"Come on and get some breakfast." Meme smiled. "You can play with her after you eat."

We had whole wheat pancakes. After I helped Meme do the breakfast dishes, I put on my tennis shoes and started outside.

"Going to go play with the puppy?" Meme called when I opened the screen.

I stopped and stood there for a moment, with my hand on the screen, staring down at the puppy. She wiggled so wild and hard, I thought she might tie herself in a knot.

Puppies are sneaky animals. Sure—they look sweet and innocent. In reality, they're sneaky, conniving little creatures that try to worm their way into your heart. They want to play, cuddle, and make you fall in love with them. Then they get sick. Then they're gone and all you have left is the hurt. I wasn't going to let that happen—no matter what.

"No," I answered. My voice was more abrupt and sharp than I'd planned. "I'm getting in shape for softball. She would just slow me down. Maybe later."

Meme's eyes narrowed.

"Stay on the place." She sighed. "Don't go out in the road."

I jogged around the outside of the fence. The dog followed me, on the inside, yapping at every step I took. Then I sprinted to the edge of the barn. Once I was out of sight, I'd figured the pup would quiet down, but she didn't. Behind the barn, I found one of Dandy's old trails and followed it.

All I could think about was Dandy. Everything reminded me of her: the trails that I followed were made by her wandering around her pasture. The piles of dried horse apples—they were hers. There was the old tree where she always stood.

I'd wanted a happy day—I didn't want to get all teary and mope around, thinking about her.

I turned my attention back to my running. On a long, flat stretch of trail I sprinted as fast as I could, then slowed to a jog. On another flat area I hit another all-out sprint. Then . . .

My stomach didn't feel so good. I walked back to the barn.

I opened the door and grabbed one of Uncle Cody's old softballs from the shelf.

The roof of the old barn was the perfect place to practice. The ridges in the tin kept the ball rolling straight.

The tin made a *clank* sound when the ball hit, then a metallic rattle as it rolled down. I caught it. Threw it back again. Caught it. Threw it—

There was no time for sad thoughts about Dandy. No time to worry about the puppy. Just throw the ball. Catch the ball. Up. Down. Don't lose it. Careful. Now, throw it a little farther. Now . . .

"What ya doin'?"

The voice startled me.

"I don't want to be boyfriend/girlfriend or anything like that."

The sound of the ball rattling down the tin roof stopped. I looked up just as the thing clunked me on the forehead.

"I just want to see the puppy."

It was Matt Green.

chapter 9

"How did you get here?" Despite the bump on my head, I tried to act cool.

"Bicycle." Matt's forehead crinkled. "You okay? I didn't mean to scare you."

"You didn't scare me," I lied. "People always sneak up on me when I'm practicing. What are you doing here?"

"Ummm. I just want to see your new pup." Matt's eyes looked into mine, but for just a second.

Picking the ball up off the ground, he held it out to me.

"There are lots of other dogs around. Why do you want to see this one?" I snatched the ball from his hand.

"Isn't this one of the Harris's pups? They have really good dogs." Matt shifted his weight from one foot to the other.

"How do you know so much about the Harris's dogs?"

"My dad said that your grandfather was bragging about the new puppy. Mom's old cocker spaniel, Goldie, died about two months ago. Dad has Rocket, but he is strictly for farmwork . . . you know—a cow dog. So we're sort of looking for a new one. Is it here or at your house?"

Ignoring him, I threw the ball back on the roof.

"Is it here?"

This time, I caught the ball. "Do your parents know where you are?"

"I was supposed to call and let them know that I got here. Can I use the phone?"

"*May* I use the phone," I corrected.

"Reckon since you know where it is, you may. But when you're done with it, can I use it?"

My eyes rolled. I couldn't tell if Matt was being a smart aleck, or if he was really that dumb.

When I didn't say anything, Matt kind of shrugged his shoulders. "Didn't your grandpa tell you that I was coming? I was supposed to call when I got here, and when I'm ready to go home I'm supposed to call again. Dad is coming after me in the truck."

"No, he didn't tell me. Nobody told me anything." My cheeks felt a little warm. "There's a phone on the patio. I'll show you."

I lead Matt toward the gate. The dog began yelping at us from the backyard.

As soon as I lifted the latch, Matt—I mean Mattie—raced through the opening. She made two high-speed circles around Matt and me, then came back and started jumping against my leg. Matt knelt down. As soon as his knees touched the ground, the pup was all over him.

Her front paws shoved at his chest. Matt laughed. I tried to look stern, but I couldn't keep the smile off my face. That little puppy had Matt helplessly trapped.

"What a great dog!"

"There's the phone to call your dad." I pointed to the metal table on the patio. "Do you need some help?"

"Nah. She's just playing. What's her name?"

"Ma-ma-Mattie," I stammered. My mind raced as I tried to explain. "She comes to Matt . . . uh . . . Mattie. She named herself."

Matt looked up at me, but he kept rubbing the little ball of fluff.

"*Matt*ie?"

"She—she wandered off the other day, and I started calling out names. She just sort of came to Ma—er, Mattie."

Matt gave me a weird look, then turned his attention back to the pup. He flopped Mattie on her back and rubbed her tummy. She let him examine her legs and chest. "This dog has great conformation. She could be a show dog."

"You better call your folks," I said, motioning him toward the table.

Matt picked up the pup in his left arm and held her against his side. He leaned away from her, trying to escape the long wet tongue that kept slopping the side of his face.

As soon as he started talking, I slipped into the house and closed the door behind me.

"Meme!" I screeched. "What's this guy doing here?"

Papa poked his head around the corner. "You mean Matt?"

I leaned against the back door, holding it shut.

"I'm sorry. Do I need to introduce you? It's Matt Green . . . from just down the road. I thought you knew each other." Papa's eyes sparkled.

"I know him. What is he doing in the yard? He said you knew he was coming here."

Papa shrugged.

"His folks are thinking about getting a new dog. Matt wanted to see your pup. His mom and dad are coming over a little bit later. Is he causing you a problem, Squirt?" Papa moved toward me.

I reached for the dead bolt, then stopped. "Nothing I can't take care of. Just warn me the next time."

"Sorry. When they called you were already outdoors. Besides, I thought you needed to study this weekend. Did you get that book read last night?" Papa's eyes caught mine.

"I'll take care of it as soon as I get rid of Matt."

I eased the door open and slid outside. Matt and the puppy were no place in sight. Walking to the back gate, I stopped. Listened. Out near the barn, I could hear Matt yelling for the pup.

"Hey, where are you going with my dog?"

"I was just checking to see how well you had her trained." Matt turned back toward the house; Mattie was right at his heels.

"I just got her—she's not trained at all. Bring her back to the yard."

"No sweat, Curly Sue." Matt reached for the gate latch.

"Do not . . . I repeat . . . do *not* call me Curly Sue—ever again! Do you understand?" I could feel the heat almost burning at the tips of my ears.

"Are you serious? What's the big deal?" Matt yanked on the gate. I held the latch down.

"My name is Kristine, and that is what I want to be called. Get it?"

"I didn't mean anything. Your grandpa calls you 'Squirt.' What's the difference?"

"Big difference . . . and you know it."

"Serious, Kristine. I didn't mean to hurt your feelings. The other day while I was waiting for the bus, somebody drove by and splashed me. When I got on the bus, somebody called me Splatty Matty. It's no big deal."

"Then apologize," I demanded.

"Is your hair curly?" Matt folded his arms and got that cocky look on his face.

"No. It's just . . . linearly challenged." I tried to keep a straight face.

Matt burst out laughing. "I can't believe you said that. That's great."

It took all the concentration I had to keep the stern, mad look on my face. "A-P-O-L-O-G-I-Z-E!" I spelled.

"N-O P-R-O-B-L-E-M! I'm sorry. Really, Kristine. I didn't mean to make you mad."

"I accept." I took my hand off the latch and let him back in. "But you *did* mean to make me mad. You were trying to look big around the other guys."

Matt folded his arms and looked down his nose

at me. "And just what were you doing when you called me a stinky fur ball?' I didn't hear anybody A-P-O-L-O-G-I-Z-E about calling me that."

"You're right. I apologize for calling you a fur ball. What I should have said was—"

"Any problems out there?" Papa called from the back door.

"Uh . . . I don't think so." Matt looked a bit worried when he glanced back at me. "Are there, Kristine?"

"Things are okay, Papa. I'm just trying to talk to Matt."

"Good. Here, Squirt, give the puppy her food and run some fresh water in her bowl." Papa set the dog dish on the back porch and closed the door.

Matt's eyes twinkled. I could just hear him thinking *Curly Sue.*

"Make yourself useful." I pointed at the bowl. "The puppy chow is in that big barrel. Don't give her too much."

I went to get water while Matt got the food. Mattie couldn't decide whether to go with me or him, so she raced back and forth between us.

We set the bucket and the food under the tree. Mattie skidded to a stop and bumped her head on the bowl, before she finally settled down to eat her food.

"I'll get some chairs," I said.

"I'll get them." Matt raced to get ahead of me.

"The chairs are hanging up in the back of the shed." I pointed to the pile of folding chairs in the corner.

Matt lifted two chairs from the pegs. I closed the door while he placed the chairs near Mattie.

"When are you getting your dog?" I scrunched down in the chair and propped my feet against the tree trunk.

"Don't know." He scratched Mattie behind her ears. "This is a neat dog."

"I'd give her to you, if I wouldn't get in trouble." My chest hurt.

"Really? I would *love* to have this dog. She is perfect. Good bloodlines. Active. Curious. Sweet." He lifted her onto his lap.

"I would, but Papa would be really mad."

"What's the matter with you and this dog, anyway?"

Mattie settled down on Matt's chest, closed her eyes, and let out a big sigh.

"She's just a pest. She makes messes and yaps all night."

"That's what puppies do, silly. Look at her now. All calm and peaceful. See how sweet she is." Matt squished up the loose skin on her neck and rubbed behind her ears.

"Yeah, but what happens later?" I stared out at the yard.

"She gets bigger and better." Careful not to bother the pup, Matt propped his legs against the tree next to mine. I moved my feet away and shook my head.

"No. You don't understand. Like when she gets old. When she gets sick or crippled or . . . you know . . . when she dies."

"We've lost pets." Matt shrugged. "It's pretty hard, but things just work that way. You really miss 'em. But after a time, it's not so bad."

I dropped my feet from the tree and shifted my weight in the chair. "Yeah, right. But after *time,* you get another pet, and it happens all over again."

Matt nodded. "It hurts when you lose a pet." He didn't look at me when he spoke. "In your head, you still remember things. You look for them in places where they should be—only . . . well, they just aren't there anymore. And you wish they were, but—but they're not."

I stared at him. For an instant I caught his eye, but he quickly looked down once more. I'd felt like I was the only one in the whole wide world who felt that way.

"Dandy, our old horse. She's in my mind's eye. That's what Meme calls it. There are times I can almost see her."

"Well you got to ride her, some. She was a gentle horse. I remember coming over one day when your grandpa was trimming her hooves. She was about as calm and sweet as any old horse I ever saw. Think about the good times." He nodded at the pup. "Look at this cute puppy. She's here *now*. You'd have to be pretty stupid to miss your time with this cool little dog, just so you can think sad thoughts about a horse you can't bring back."

Thinking about Dandy—thinking about when I was little and Papa used to lead her around the lot and let me ride her—thinking about lying on her back while he trimmed her hooves—all those thoughts that rustled through my head like a fresh spring breeze, almost brought a smile to my face. There *were* good thoughts, but . . . suddenly my mind took another turn.

Did Matt just call me stupid? I sat straight up and glared at him.

"You think I'm stupid?"

chapter 10

Something furry tickled my cheek. I cracked open one sleepy eye. Mattie wiggled, sighed, and snuggled closer. The morning sun streaked through the blinds in my bedroom, leaving strips of light and shadow on the wall. It was way too early to get up. My eyes shut.

Matt's face appeared in the darkness. My cheeks warmed as I remembered how he called me stupid. Luckily for him, his mom and dad had driven up just in time to save him. Then they'd all looked over the pup and bragged on her. Mr. Green and Papa talked about the weather, how the crops were doing, and how bad the grasshoppers were supposed to be this next summer. Usual farmer stuff. Mostly they'd talked about Mattie and what a *fine* dog she was.

Matt did apologize before he left. He was nice

about it. I smiled. Mattie was now stretched out on her back, with her legs in the air and her little head turned toward me. Her tongue flicked out to lick me. I giggled.

In the blink of an eye, Mattie leaped to her feet and started jumping around the bed. I grabbed her and held her. She started squirming, and I realized that she needed out—now!

The pup raced in circles as I stumbled down the hall.

"I'm hurrying as fast as I can."

"Wait, Kristine," Meme called from the kitchen doorway. "Take her out the back. I don't know how well she will come when you call her. She doesn't really know her name yet, and I don't have time to chase her right now. You don't look like you're awake enough to chase her, either."

"Okay." I yawned. Mattie raced past me as we hurried to the back door. As soon as I opened the screen, she shot outside.

"Do you have Apple Jacks, or has Papa eaten all of them?"

"You're in luck, kid. He hasn't found them, yet."

The front door closed. Papa's work boots clopped across the living room floor. "Okay to let the pup in?"

Before I could think of an excuse, Meme said, "Not yet. She hasn't been out very long."

Papa's hopeful look vanished.

"I'm sorry I brought that dog home!"

Meme rushed across the room toward him. "Larry, I need to speak with you, outside."

Papa grabbed his cap and stuffed it on his head. "That Green boy would give his right arm to have a pup like that. Wish I'd given it to him! I wish—"

Meme pulled him toward the back door. "Larry, hush."

"He's just cranky," Meme said when she came back. "He had trouble getting the tractor started this morning, and the ground wasn't ready to disk when he got to the field. Just farm stuff." Yet I couldn't help but notice her worried look as she walked to the window to watch.

"Kristine."

The sound of my name startled me. Meme stood by my chair. "I need some help with the flower beds."

I pulled myself out of the recliner. "Do you have extra gloves?"

"Check that drawer by the sink."

I found the gloves and followed her outside.

"I want this area ready to replant." Meme stayed busy, but she kept turning her head as if waiting for something.

"Was Papa mad at me?" I finally asked.

"He wanted you to like that pup. He's hurt that you don't. What is it, anyway?"

I sighed. "She's okay. There's just other stuff going on. Mom. The baby. You know."

"There is a lot going on, but that pup is aching to have you love her. I'm not sure how you can resist. She's already nearly housebroken, and she is a great cuddler." Meme kept her head down.

"She's cute, but I don't have time for a pup. A dog takes up a lot of time. I have responsibilities."

"That sounds very mature. But I don't buy it for a second."

Suddenly, my cheeks felt awfully hot.

Without so much as a glance in my direction, Meme dug another weed. "There has to be something else. That dog is as sweet as she can be." Meme finally looked up from the weeds and stared me straight in the eye. "So, what's really going on?"

"Nothing. Honest." I tried to look away, but her eyes held mine.

"Nothing?" Meme reached over to touch my hand.

"Everything, I guess." I tried to smile back, but it didn't work. "She *is* sweet, she's cute as can be. I just—just . . ."

"Are you afraid of losing her?" Meme's voice was soft.

My head jerked around to look at her. "H-how did you know?"

Meme sat quiet for a moment. "Kristine, I know how it feels to lose a pet. I know how it feels to lose a person you love. My mother died three years before you were born. That was very painful and I thought the hurt would never go away. But I have so many wonderful memories of her."

"I'm sorry. I don't want you to be sad."

"No, you don't get it, Kristine. There *are* sad things. But the happy things—the good things— outweigh them. You have to give the good a chance, though!

"Each person or animal that comes into our lives, stays with us forever." She tapped a finger against her chest. "They stay in here. And when they're taken away, we shouldn't rage at God or curse the world because they are gone. We shouldn't regret that they were here. We should remember them and the joy they brought us." Meme started digging again.

The rumble of the tractor made us look up.

"We're done for now, Kristine," she called over her shoulder. "If you still need to read that book for your report next week, this would be a great time to work on it."

"Sure."

When Meme took me home, Papa was playing tug-of-war with Mattie. Even Papa agreed that a new puppy would be an inconvenience the first few days a new baby was home.

I sat in Kate's room and read my book while she napped. Then Grandma and Grandpa Rankin brought Anna home for the afternoon.

Anna was excited to have Kate in the house. She brought her favorite toys and put them in the crib. When it was time to feed Kate, Mama held her in one arm. Anna sat on Mama's knee, holding her favorite doll just like Mama held Kate. But it wasn't long before Anna got restless, so I took her to the playroom where we dressed and undressed her dolls. I forgot about Dandy. I forgot about Mattie and Matt. For a while, I forgot all about everything.

When Grandma Rankin came to get Anna, she asked if I wanted to go with them, but it felt good to be home, so I didn't go. After they left, Daddy and I fixed bacon, lettuce, and tomato sandwiches.

Mama came to sit with us while we ate. "Do you think we need to go get the pup, Kristine?" she asked.

"Ah . . . I think she's okay there. Why, did Papa call?"

Mama gave me a funny look and shook her head. "No. I talked to Mother. She said that the pup was lonesome. She's moping around the house looking for you."

"Don't you think it would be better if we waited until Kate was more used to the house? You know, before we bring in a wild puppy tearing all over the place?"

Mama frowned.

"It might be better if the dog was already here when Anna comes home tomorrow," Daddy said, carrying the plates to the sink.

"Can't we wait another day?" Keeping my eyes down, I wiped the table.

"Is that what you want to do?" Daddy asked.

"Sure. I can get caught up on my sleep. I have to finish reading a book. It'll be a lot easier without her here. We'll just wait until tomorrow, okay?"

Mama stood up. I could feel her eyes on me. "Is there something going on, Kristine?" she asked finally.

"Nope. Just schoolwork. Well . . . that . . . and a brand new baby." I sounded so innocent and casual, I almost believed myself. Mama didn't move. I turned around, reached over, and stroked Kate's little head. "Isn't she tiny? Isn't she *so* sweet?"

Mama sighed. "Well, maybe Kristine's right. The puppy might bark at night. We could use a few days to settle in."

"You know what?" Daddy leaned back. "That pup is used to a big yard at your mom and dad's. I've been thinking . . ."

"Yes?" One of Mama's eyebrows raised.

"I've been thinking about putting up a privacy fence. Puppy could use the room. I'll call Garrison's and see how much it would cost, and how long it will take them to get it up. What do you think?"

Mama smiled. "As long as it's not too expensive."

"I'll go call, right now." Daddy smiled back.

It worked out great. Now instead of having an extra day without the pup, I had at least a week. I couldn't have been happier.

On Monday, Coach's little boy was sick, so we had regular PE. The substitute teacher put four classes together and let us play dodgeball.

Everybody loved dodgeball—especially the boys.

When it was just the girls, we practiced softball skills. Since we were all together . . . well, dodgeball was fun.

Matt was on the other team. Two of the boys on our team tried to put him out. One threw his ball at Matt's feet. He jumped it. At the same time the other guy threw straight at him. Matt caught the ball before his feet even touched the ground.

When I got the ball again, I sneaked to the line—trying to act invisible so I could peg players when they weren't looking. Out of the corner of my eye, I saw Matt streaking toward me.

"Hey, Kristine. No hard feelings, right?"

"What are you talking about?" I asked.

"Saturday? You know, when I said you were stupid. Only I really didn't say you were stupid. It wasn't what I meant. I'm—ah—er . . ." He stammered. "I'm trying to apologize—okay? I wasn't trying to hurt your feelings or anything like that. I just think it's stupid not to enjoy that new puppy."

"Oh, no problem." I let out a little laugh. "I've already forgotten about it."

The smile stretched clear across Matt's face. He turned his attention to one of the boys on my team who was standing near the midline. As soon as he started for him, I drew back my ball and threw it as hard as I could.

In all the years we played dodgeball at school, I never threw such a perfect ball. The thing went *BLAP*—right upside Matt Green's head. It hit him so hard, he dropped his ball, staggered a few steps to the side, then fell. He rolled and scrambled right back to his feet. Blinking and cross-eyed, his mouth fell open when he turned to look at me.

I gave him my most angelic smile and raced off to get another ball.

Revenge is sweet!

chapter 11

"Is he still there?" I didn't dare look.

Selena, who was standing almost nose to nose with me, leaned a little to the side.

"He's still watching."

Suddenly she let out a little snort. I wanted to turn around so bad, it hurt. But I didn't dare.

"What is it? Selena? What?"

She snorted again and tried to wipe the smile off her face. "He's not watching now!"

"Why?"

"Somebody passed him the ball, but Matt was watching you instead of thinking about the game. Thing swished by, less than an inch from his ear, and he didn't even see it! The other guys are punching him right now."

* * *

I didn't see much of Matt for the rest of the day. When the bell finally rang, I grabbed my stuff and waited for Selena. We walked down the hall. Almost at the back door, she stopped dead in her tracks.

"Where are you going? You're not riding the bus today. Your mom's home with the baby."

"Daddy's picking me up."

"Oh." Selena took about five more steps, then stopped again. "I wish I didn't have to ride the bus. I wish I could go home with you and play with the baby."

We walked on. Again we didn't get more than five steps. This time, *I* was the one who stopped. That was because Mrs. Peck stuck her head out of the office.

"Kristine."

"Yes, ma'am."

"Your dad called. Said he'd be about five minutes late. You know where to meet him, right?"

"Yes, ma'am."

"If he doesn't come pretty quick, you come back to the office and let me know. Okay?"

"Okay."

Except for a second grader who forgot his homework, Selena was the last one on the bus. Mrs.

Martin held the door handle and cocked an eyebrow at me.

"Dad's picking me up," I explained.

As the bus pulled away, I waved at Selena. The next thing I knew, I was staring straight up at Matt Green. Even with his cheek pressed against the bus window, he still had that weird look on his face, puzzled and confused.

It was all I could do to keep from laughing.

Daddy was four minutes late. Not five.

"Sorry," he said. "The men from the fence company showed up. I wasn't paying attention to the time."

"You mean they've already started on the fence?" I tried not to sound too disappointed.

Oh, great! Now I've only got a couple of days without the puppy.

I thought that, but I didn't say it. Instead, I said: "Oh, that's fast. I can hardly wait."

Mama and Kate were asleep when we got home. Both Daddy and I were really quiet—until . . . Daddy tried to get the big pan that Mama used for boiling corn out of the cabinet. When he pulled on it, two smaller pans fell out and rattled around on the floor.

"All right. What's going on in there?" Mama called.

"Nothing," he answered. "Kristine and I are fixing supper. You go back to sleep." Daddy put water in the pan while I got some ears of corn from the freezer. "Think it's supposed to come to a boil before we put in the corn," he said. "Let's go out back and see how the men did on the fence today."

I opened the glass storm door and stepped outside. Daddy followed.

The backyard *did* look a little different. There were shiny silver poles sticking up at regular intervals all around the edge. I started down the steps to take a closer look when:

WHAM!

The loud noise made me jump. I spun around. Daddy spun around, too. He looked at the door a moment, then opened it—just a bit—before he let it go.

Wham!

Frowning, he opened it once more. From the other room, I could hear Kate crying. This time he put a hand between the door and the door jam. The instant he let it go, the thing tried to slam again.

"Here," he said, dropping to one knee. "Hold the door for me. Think the door-closer is messed up."

"Door-closer? What's that?"

"This cylinder-looking thing. When you open the door the silver rod sucks air into the cylinder. When you let go, the gaskets inside let the air out slowly. Supposed to keep the door from slamming shut. I just need to adjust it."

He started twisting a little knob that stuck out from the cylinder thing.

"Already tried that."

We both looked up. Mama stood there, holding Kate.

"Thought you were taking a nap."

"Who can sleep with you two clanging pans and slamming the door?" Mama tried to look mean, but her eyes were twinkling and a sly smile curled the corners of her mouth.

Daddy twisted the little knob a few more times, then motioned me to let go of the door. The thing swished shut so fast, it almost knocked him over.

"Well, guess your mom's right. Thing's worn out. I'll run by the hardware store tomorrow and pick up a new one."

When Daddy and I inspected the silver poles in the yard, I tried to jiggle one. It wouldn't move. The concrete was already hard. My shoulders sagged.

At this rate, I'd be stuck with that dog a whole lot sooner than I wanted.

chapter 12

Daddy never made it to pick up the door-closer on Tuesday. Both Mama and I reminded him, but he ended up working for one of his clients and didn't get finished until late. I thought about it during the day, but right before the bell rang, we had to turn in our votes for the Legs Contest.

Wednesday morning, I *did* remind him, only it was after I got out of the car and he was driving off. I wasn't sure he'd heard me.

When I got inside school, each class came up with one list they agreed upon for the Legs Contest. Then the whole school went to the gym.

At the assembly program, the eighth graders won.

Our class would have won, but we placed Mr. Arrington with the fuzzy slippers and Mrs. McMasters with the combat boots. Some of the boys in our class booed and claimed the teachers had cheated. Mr. Wheat marched up to the front of the stage with that "mean principal look" on his face, folded his arms, and glared down at our boys. They shut up *real quick.*

"Mrs. Horrell, did you help your class with their voting?"

"No, sir. I did not."

"Mr. Arrington. Did you tell anyone in the eighth grade which legs belonged to you?"

"No, sir. Absolutely not!"

I couldn't help notice the grin that replaced the "mean principal look" on Mr. Wheat's face. "Then, perhaps, Mr. Arrington, you can explain to the students how—"

"Oh, I can! I can!" Lisa Parnell leaped to her feet and waved her arm around like she was fighting off a swarm of bumblebees. Lisa was probably the most popular eighth-grade girl in the whole school. She was the star first baseman on the softball team—the girl everyone knew would be chosen for the State All Star Team.

Mr. Wheat held out his hand toward her.

"Be my guest, Miss Parnell."

Lisa looked very proud of herself.

"Mr. Arrington shaved his legs!"

"Yuck!" A bunch of the fifth- and sixth-grade boys gasped. Mr. Wheat tried to look serious.

"Just how did you figure that out, young lady?" Mr. Arrington asked. "I've never worn shorts to school. Not this year, anyway."

Lisa's smile stretched even bigger.

"When you shave your legs and the hair starts growing back, it itches. We noticed that in the lunchroom, every time you got your tray and sat down, you'd reach under the table and scratch."

"Yeah," an eighth-grade boy added. "There were a couple of times we thought you were gonna dig a hole in your legs."

Mr. Arrington's face turned a bright shade of red. He gave a helpless shrug and quickly sat back down in his folding chair. Then . . .

He leaned over and scratched his legs. He overacted, making a big show of it.

The whole gym burst into laughter. (Well, everyone but the kindergartners and first graders. They just kind of sat there, with their mouths opened, wondering what was going on.)

"I still think it's cheating," Selena pouted. "I mean, we're just fifth graders. How are we supposed to know about shaving your legs? It's not fair."

Before Daddy picked me up, Selena asked if I could come spend Friday night at her house and bring the puppy. I told her that the puppy was still at Meme and Papa's.

"Besides, I need to study."

When I got home, most of the fence was finished. The only things missing were a gate at the side of the house and the big double gate at the back. Daddy told Mama that they would put the gates up tomorrow or the day after. "Kristine will have to wait another day or two before she can have her puppy," he added.

Great! How lucky can I be?

.

It was going to be *my* dinner this evening. I had five beautifully shaped salmon patties on the griddle and was just ready to pour the taters-n-onions into the skillet, when we heard a bloodcurdling scream from the living room. We all got there at the same time. Anna was lying under the rocking chair.

Daddy yanked the chair off her and gently picked her up in his arms. He looked her over, then held her out to Mama.

"She's fine," Mama said finally. "She was just scared because she was pinned down and couldn't get up."

Mama spun Anna back around so she was facing her. "Were you climbing on the back of the rocking chair again, Anna?"

Anna ducked her head.

"Anna?" Daddy's voice was more stern than Mama's.

Guilt covered Anna's face like a blanket. Her bottom lip pooched out so far, a parakeet could have perched on it. She nodded her head.

"That's what I thought." Daddy gave her a big hug. "Come with me—we'll find something for you to play with."

Just then the doorbell rang.

Daddy opened the door. A couple of men stood there. One man flipped his thumb toward their truck. "I know it's a little late, Mr. Rankin. But we got those gates finished. If it's okay with you, we'll go ahead and put them up."

Daddy glanced down at his watch.

"It's six thirty. You fellas usually work this late?"

"No, sir." He smiled. "We finished early with the job we were working on and went back to the shop. We managed to get the gates finished and . . . well . . . ah . . ."

The other man shrugged.

"Well, we know the fence was for your daughter's new puppy."

"Yeah," the younger man broke in. "Ain't no sense keeping that little girl and her puppy apart. So . . ."

"Yeah. It'll just take a couple of minutes to install them. If it's all right with you."

Daddy shook both of the men's hands. "This is really nice of you guys. I just can't tell you how much we appreciate this. Kristine will be so happy."

I tried my best to smile when they looked at me. It took so much effort, it almost hurt.

I guess it worked. They smiled back, then scurried off toward their truck. Daddy turned to Mama.

"Reckon we should ask them to stay for supper?" he said softly.

Mama's eyes flashed wide.

"Supper!" she repeated.

That's when the smoke alarm went off.

chapter 13

Smoke alarms are loud, shrill, and scary. Mama pushed Anna at me. Okay—it's more like she tossed her. I managed to catch her and we raced after Mama when she ran for the kitchen.

Grease fires aren't loud. Grease fires aren't shrill. But they *are* the scariest thing in the world.

Yellow-orange flames leaped from the center of the big black frying pan. Grayish black smoke bellowed up. The fire seemed to lap at the bottom of the cabinet above the range.

Mama rushed to the stove, opened the cabinet, and grabbed something. Without the least bit of fear, she slipped a big lid over the top of the blazing skillet. A streak of flames climbed from the burner and up the side. Then there was nothing but smoke, oozing from the small crack between the lid and the black pan.

Mama waited a moment, until she was sure the fire was out and all the burners were off. Then she grabbed a hot pad and carefully scooted the skillet and the griddle off the hot burners.

"Richard. I'll open the window. Take Kate and Anna outside. They don't need to be in all this smoke."

The door banged shut when Mama came outside to join us. She shot it a look, then smiled at me. I could feel the tears start to well up in my eyes.

"I'm sorry, Mama." I fought to keep from crying. "I forgot to turn the burner down. It's all my fault. I'm—"

"It's not your fault." She leaned so close, her nose was almost touching mine. "Stuff like that just happens. It's not anybody's fault. Do you understand?"

"Yes . . . yes, ma'am."

Mama hugged me. "Keep your cool. Use your head. And . . ." She paused, glancing over her shoulder. Sure that Daddy was still busy watching the fence guys, she smiled back at me. "Your dad is one of the most intelligent men I know. But when it comes to a kitchen fire . . ." She let out a sigh, then shook her head. "Back when we were dating, we decided to pop some popcorn one evening. Meme and Papa were already asleep. Your dad put the grease on to heat up. While we were waiting, we decided—to—ah—er—" she stammered.

I could tell that whatever it was they "decided," Mama wasn't ready to talk to me about it. Must be one of those "Wait till you're older" type deals.

"There was a full moon that night," she went on. "We thought we should go outside and look at it. When we came back inside, the pan was blazing and your dad poured some water in the pitcher. If I hadn't stopped him, he would have burned the whole house down."

Mama started toward where Daddy, Kate, and Anna were watching the men put the finishing touches on the gate, but stopped when she realized I wasn't following.

"What is it, Kristine?"

"I don't get it, Mama."

"You mean about putting the fire out?"

"No. About the popcorn. I didn't think you were supposed to put pots and pans in the microwave. And why did Daddy put grease in a pan, instead of just putting the package in?"

Mama didn't answer. She just stood there, with her mouth hanging open, for a long, long time. Finally, she blinked, and went over to where Daddy was watching the men. She whispered something to him. Daddy turned to look at me, then let out a little chuckle.

I asked again about the popcorn. When I did, Mama and Daddy both started snickering. "We'll show you how we did things in the *old days,*" was all they would say.

It was just getting dark when we got to Meme C's house. I kept my eyes straight ahead as we drove up the gravel road to the house. If I looked in the pasture, the memories would try to sneak back into my head.

Meme gave Anna a big hug. She gave Kate a gentle kiss on the cheek. Then she looked square at me.

"Is this the child you were telling me about? The one who's never had *real* popcorn?"

Mama nodded.

"This is the one."

I felt like a total idiot. I had no idea why they were making fun of me. So I just stood there and shifted uncomfortably from one foot to the other. Meme C took my hand and led me to the kitchen. She pulled a small pan from beneath the stove, placed it on the counter, and knelt back down.

"Turn the front left burner on to about medium,"

she said. There was more rattling while she searched for the lid.

I reached for the knob, then hesitated. We had an electric range, but Meme C had a gas stove. It always startled me when I turned it on! The flames would shoot up—all blue—and make a popping sound. After this evening, I did *not* want to mess with fire in any way, shape, or form. Mama and Daddy stood at the doorway to the kitchen. Their smiles were a little unnerving—in fact, kind of irritating. When I didn't turn the stove on, Mama folded her arms and arched her eyebrows.

I turned the knob. The thing hissed, then popped, as the ring of blue flames ignited.

Beside the range, Meme had placed a beat-up looking little pan, a bent lid, measuring spoons, and a glass jar full of . . . of . . . well, I guess it was popcorn. I mean, it wasn't like I'd never seen popcorn before. But these things were what was left in the bottom of the sack after you finished. They were the hard little yellow chunks.

Then Meme set the cooking oil on the cabinet.

And . . . I didn't *want* to handle it.

Fact was—I flat refused!

chapter 14

I truly wasn't trying to act like a total snot. I was just scared.

At first Meme, Daddy, and Mama laughed and teased me a little. Then they tried to encourage me, telling me over and over again that it was perfectly safe.

Trouble was, the more they talked and tried to convince me . . . well, the worse it got.

I probably would have never cooked "real" popcorn in my whole entire life, if it hadn't been for Papa.

Everyone thought he was still in front of the TV—sound asleep. He suddenly stomped into the kitchen, shoved between Mama and Daddy, practically knocking them out of the doorway, and clomped across the floor.

"Been sittin' in there for thirty minutes, waitin' on some popcorn," he snarled—his gruff voice more like a growl. "All I hear is talk, talk, talk. Don't hear no popcorn poppin'. Don't even smell popcorn. I'll just pop the darned stuff myself!"

Then he whirled around to glare at Meme, Mama, and Daddy. "Get on outa here," he grumbled.

"But we're trying to teach Kristine how to—" Meme started.

"Don't care what you're tryin' to do," he snorted, cutting her off. "I'm gonna fix myself some popcorn. Now get!"

In a huff, Meme stomped across the floor. Her feet hit almost as hard and loud as Papa's had. Everyone disappeared into the living room. I started to follow them, when Papa grabbed my arm.

His big hard calloused hands felt as gentle as Kate's baby touch. I looked up at him. His eyes sparkled.

"You stay put," he whispered. "Let me show you how this works."

He motioned me closer, glanced at the doorway, and put a finger to his lips. "Okay, first off what you do is put two tablespoons of cooking oil in the pan. Then . . ."

"We had a fire today, Papa. I don't want to be around cooking oil. And that little pan . . ."

He stuck his finger to his lips, shushing me again.

"I know all about that. And you can probably tell, just by lookin', that this pan's been scorched a time or two. But I'm gonna show you how to do it *right*. But you got to pay attention." He glanced over his shoulder again. "And, you gotta keep quiet. I don't want them knowing my secrets."

He repeated: "Two tablespoons of oil." Then he set the pot on the stove.

"That's the part I don't like, Papa. Putting it over the fire and—"

"Shut! Up!"

It's amazing how soft he could whisper—but how loud it seemed to bounce around in my head.

"Now get me three kernels of popcorn. Don't rattle the jar when you open it."

Keeping my arm far away from the heat, I started to drop them in.

"You're not a high-altitude bomber pilot," he whispered. "Don't drop 'em from the ceiling. Just put 'em in."

I was so busy trying to be quiet, I forgot to be scared. Papa motioned me next to him with a jerk of his head.

He nodded toward the stove.

"In a minute or two, you'll hear those kernels pop. That means it's ready. Then I'll lift the lid, and you'll pour a quarter cup of popcorn in. Fill that measuring cup on the counter. Then we'll be all ready to—"

A little *thump* made Papa stop, right in the middle of what he was saying. A second or two later, the *thump* came again. Papa nodded toward the measuring cup. When I picked it up and turned back to him, he didn't lift the lid.

"Always wait about ten to fifteen seconds," he whispered. "Sometimes that third kernel won't pop along with the others. Sometimes, it won't even pop at all."

As we waited, I could see his lips moving, like he was counting to himself. Finally, he nodded and lifted the lid. Quiet as I could, I poured the popcorn into the pan. Papa set it back on the stove.

Noises started coming from inside the pan—*thunks* that whacked the lid, and almost seemed to make it bounce. Papa shook or slid the pan back and forth on the range. "Here," he said, stuffing the pot holder in my hand. "You shake while I find the bowl to put it in. Keep shaking so the popcorn won't stick. Try to keep it quiet, if you can."

I was so busy trying to be quiet . . . well, I poured the second batch of white fluffy popcorn into the bowl—without even realizing that I was the one who popped it.

"One more batch ought to do it," Papa whispered. "I'll melt some butter."

I poured two tablespoons of cooking oil into the pan. Dropped in the three kernels and set it on the stove. Then I folded my arms and turned to glare at Papa. He didn't notice at first. He got a big chunk of butter from the fridge and plopped it in a glass measuring cup. He set it in the microwave and closed the door. When he punched the timer, it beeped.

"Take *your* popcorn out before you pour butter on it," Meme called from the other room. "You remember what the doctor said about your heart and eating too much butter and salt."

Papa folded his arms and glared at the empty doorway. "That old woman's ears work better than the sonar on a submarine. How did she hear that little ole beep?"

That's when he realized I was glaring at him, just like he was glaring at Meme.

"What?"

"How did you do that?"

"How did I do what?"

"Make me fix the popcorn—without even knowing I was the one doing it."

I expected him to grin or chuckle about tricking me. He didn't. He just leaned forward and looked at the butter in the microwave.

"*I* didn't do it. *You* did it—all by yourself." He nodded at the popcorn. "Keep shakin'.

"You were just a little nervous, on account of the fire this evening. When you were little, your mom used to set you in front of her on the saddle, and take you for rides. About the time you turned five, you decided you were big enough to ride Dandy all by yourself.

"We put you on her and led her around the pen. Your grandmother watched you like a hawk. Stayed right beside you. Things went okay for about fifteen minutes, then one of those old barn cats came flying out of the doorway and shot right under Dandy's hooves. She shied—kinda took a quick step to the side—and you slid off."

That's when the smile came to his face. His eyes sparkled so much, they almost seemed to dance.

"Your grandmother swooped you up—mite near before you even bounced—and set you right back on that horse. You were so determined to ride Dandy and so busy holding on, you didn't even know how hard you hit the ground. You just concentrated on hanging on. The whole time you never so much as let out a whimper. You knew you could do it, and you wanted to do it. Same thing with the popcorn."

I'd heard the story about falling off Dandy before, but this time it made sense. As I watched him, I realized he wasn't just talking about the horse *or* the popcorn. He was talking to himself as well. That—I *didn't* understand.

With one last look at the melted butter, his bottom lip pooched out a bit. Finally he shrugged and shot a blast of air up his forehead. Then he poured the melted butter over the popcorn in the big bowl. Left the smaller bowl with nothing but popcorn in it.

"You're an excellent popcorn popper, Miss Kristine Rankin. Think we got enough to feed everybody. Turn the burner off. Let's go eat."

We tore into that popcorn like we were starving. Anna grabbed double handfuls out of the bowl. I think she ended up with more on her cheeks and mouth than she did inside her.

We talked and laughed. Meme told the story about Daddy setting the grease on fire and trying to get water to put it out. I waited until she finished, then I asked: "Just *what were* Mama and Daddy doing outside that they weren't watching the popcorn?"

Mama shot me a look. It was too late.

"Smoochin'." Papa answered without even batting an eye.

"What?" I frowned.

"Smoochin'," he repeated.

"You know," Meme said, helping him out.

"Kissing? Necking? Hugging? Smooching is an old-fashioned term for 'making out.'"

Mama's cheeks turned a little red. "How did you know?" She leaned forward and glared at Papa. "You weren't watching, were you?"

Papa held up a finger until he finished munching the last mouthful of his dry popcorn. "Don't know exactly what you two were doing. Whatever it was, you sure weren't paying attention to the popcorn."

We all laughed, visited, and finished off every last bite. When we left, Daddy held Kate, I held Anna's hand, and Mama opened the front door. She hesitated a moment, then let the screen go. It bounced shut. Smiling, she turned to Meme.

"You still have any of those turkey-bells Grandpa used to have?"

Meme nodded. "They're collectors items. Can't find the things anymore. But I think there's a few in the closet. I'll go get one."

We waited until Meme brought a small bell to her. The thing looked like one of the antique cow bells Meme kept on the mantel—only smaller.

It had been a wonderful evening. Until . . .

We said our good-byes and were just going out the door again, when Daddy stopped.

"Oh! We almost forgot the puppy!"

chapter 15

Mama came to stand beside me at the back door.

"Don't you want to let her in, so she can sleep with you tonight? Meme says she's a good snuggle puppy. She's pretty well housebroken, and—"

"No!" I shook my head—then tried my sweetest smile. "It's a nice night. I think she'll be fine outside."

"But she looks so lonely."

"I'm really tired, Mama. She might keep me awake."

Mattie hadn't even been here thirty minutes, and already she was making a liar out of me. She was sitting on the top step looking up at us. She wagged her tail a little, but didn't jump against the door. She just sat.

"Are you sure, Kristine?"

"She's fine, Mama. She needs to get used to her new home."

Before Mama could say any more, I closed the door. The turkey bell that she'd tied to the outside handle jingled. Mama said that since Daddy couldn't remember to get the door-closer, maybe the turkey bell would help.

I turned off the porch light. As I closed the inside door, I could see the dog's look. Her ears perked, as if she expected the door to open. Then her head drooped, but her eyes stayed on me. A look that seemed to say: "Why don't I get to come in? What did I do wrong?"

I shoved the door shut and turned the lock.

School was a little different now. Ever since I plastered Matt Green upside the head with the dodgeball and knocked him off his feet, I got a lot of attention. When we had girls softball practice, I was one of the first picked. If we stayed inside because of rain or something and played dodgeball, the boys usually got to be captains. They picked their friends first. But when it came down to the girls—I was always one of the first they called on.

One day when we were changing classes, Brandon Leonard passed me in the hall and said, "Hi, Kristine."

The other girls stopped and stared at me, their eyes wide and books clutched against their chests.

Brandon was probably the most popular boy in seventh grade. As soon as baseball started, he was going to be the starting pitcher. It was almost always an eighth grader who was pitcher for the team. But Brandon was so good, everyone in school knew it would be him.

Besides that, he was cute. Tall and slender, he had the most gorgeous wavy black hair I ever saw.

"He knows your name," Selena breathed.

I shrugged, trying my best to act like it was no big deal, and just kept walking.

Going to Meme and Papa's after school was something I missed. I liked listening to Papa's stories and I enjoyed his teasing. I missed the smell of fresh baked bread and cookies. And . . . in a way . . . I missed riding the bus.

I never thought I'd ever miss riding the bus.

Still, Matt was on that bus. So was Brandon Leonard and . . . well . . . as soon as things got back to normal . . . we'd see.

I *didn't miss* thinking about the old horse. In fact I went almost a whole week, and not once did a memory of her sneak in to trouble my mind.

* * *

"Go play with the puppy."

"It's time to feed the puppy."

"Don't you want to let the puppy in?"

That's all I heard. As soon as I got home, Mama or Daddy didn't ask how my day was or if I had homework or anything like that. It was always: "Puppy this. Puppy that. Puppy, puppy, puppy!"

Most times, Anna got to go along. That was fine with me. Anna kept Mattie entertained. That way, I didn't have to mess with her.

The two of them would run around the backyard. Anna would squeal and the dog would chase her. Then, sooner or later, Anna would fall down and the pup would be all over her. She'd bounce around, dart in to lick Anna's face, then bounce away again before Anna could catch her. Anna would giggle and squeal even more. Finally, she'd wrap the dog in her arms and hug her—Mattie wiggling all over and licking her anyplace she could.

Like I said, that was fine with me. The times Anna stayed inside, the stupid dog was next to impossible to get away from. She'd jump against my leg, trying to get me to pet her or play with her. I had to push her back with my foot. That was the only way to keep her from getting my pants filthy.

I have to admit—there were a few times when I

wanted to reach down and pet her. A time or two when I could hardly help from laughing at her.

But I didn't!

I wasn't about to fall for that.

It was 3:16 when I woke up.

I didn't even remember getting up.

The first thing I *did* remember was standing at my bedroom door, staring back at the bright red numbers on the digital alarm clock.

And . . .

A horrific clap of thunder made me jump. It struck so close, it shook the whole house.

I headed for Mama and Daddy's room.

Anna screamed, Kate started crying, the light came on in Mama and Daddy's room, and the door flew open—all at the same instant. Mama headed for Kate's room. Daddy went after Anna.

"You all right?" they both called.

I stood there. I hated to act like a kid—scared of a little old thunderstorm—running for the safety of Mama and Daddy's bed.

When Daddy came out, holding Anna on his hip, he paused at the doorway and held out an arm. I hesitated.

Then a third CRACK rattled the windows. I

shot to him like a streak. Anna in one arm and the other arm wrapped around my shoulder, all three of us went in and hopped on the bed. Kate rested on Mama's chest. Despite the thunder, her sleepy eyes were just barely open. Sniffling and whimpering, Anna snuggled beside them. I squeezed in next.

"Oh, shoot!" Daddy yelped. All at once he tossed the covers off, sat up, and threw his legs over the side of the bed. Before we could even ask what was wrong, he was gone.

"What happened?" I whispered.

Mama just shrugged.

From somewhere on the far side of the house, we could hear Daddy.

"Wait! Stop!" he yelled. "Come back. I've got to dry you off first."

Before it even dawned on me what he was yelling about, it hit.

A wet, wiggly, squirmy, licky, trembly pile of fur leaped over the foot of the bed and landed smack-dab in the middle of my stomach.

chapter 16

Sleeping next to a scared puppy is like sleeping during an earthquake.

Once I held Mattie beside me in the bed, so she wouldn't try to climb all over everybody, she finally calmed. But the thunder had really scared her. She shook and trembled. Then she'd stop—I guess to take a breath—and the tremors would start again.

If I took my hand away, she pushed herself, harder, against my side. Even in a king-sized bed— with five of us, there was no place to go. If I moved away from Mattie, I'd either squash Anna or push Kate and Mama off the far side of the bed.

We could hear the thunder rumbling off in the distance, but the rain kept pounding the roof. And— the pup kept shaking. I forced my eyes to stay shut and kept my hand on the dog. If I didn't get to sleep, I'd be totally shot come morning.

As if the trembling pup wasn't bad enough, Anna was no fun to sleep with, either. She flipped, flopped, twisted, jerked, and kicked me in the side a few times. Finally, when I was almost asleep, she rolled over and clunked me in the nose with her arm.

Quiet as could be, Daddy finally eased out of bed, took his pillow, and crept off to the living room. Half asleep, I tried to scoot the vibrating puppy over so we would have some more room. She wouldn't budge. I finally had to sit up in bed, pick her up, and move her. I'd hardly scooted away from Anna when Mattie shoved back against me—shaking like a leaf.

When Daddy patted the top of my head, I blinked and opened one eye.

"We overslept," he whispered, smiling down at me. "I'll fix you something for breakfast. You better hurry and get dressed."

I felt like I just got to sleep. Head fuzzy and eyes that felt like someone had poured sand in them, I sat up. Only I couldn't move. The puppy was there. Struggling and groggy, I had to climb over her. I stumbled out of bed and staggered toward the bathroom.

That silly dog never so much as opened an eye. She just snoozed away, peaceful as baby Kate.

* * *

Thursday was a total bummer.

First off, I was late to school. Mrs. McMasters didn't send me to the office for a hall pass, but she did shoot me a look when I came in during the middle of reading class. I started toward her to explain what had happened, but she pointed me to my desk with her eyes. Quietly, I sat down and opened my reader. I'd tell her later.

I didn't get to visit with Selena because I was late. So, we got in trouble during social studies for talking. Then we had a pop quiz in math. We got our papers back right before lunch.

I made a D–!

Recess was a drag, too.

Along with all the lightning, thunder, and rain, the storms that rolled through brought a warm front. Between the bright sunshine, all the moisture and humidity, not to mention no wind—it was downright hot!

Way too hot for this time of year.

When we changed classes that afternoon, I walked right past Brandon Leonard in the hall. We were so close that he almost bumped my arm. He didn't say anything. So I smiled at him and said, "Hi, Brandon."

He glanced over—sort of regarding me like I

was no more than a bug or something he passed on the playground—and kept right on walking.

Thursday was a bummer. A total bummer!

"Oh, here they are!" Mama's cheerful voice snapped me back from the awful memory of Thursday.

Thankful to be back in the present, I shook my head and focused on the picture Mama held.

"Isn't that the most darling thing you ever saw, Richard?" Mama held the picture in one hand and wrapped her free arm around Daddy. Then she wiggled the picture right in front of my nose. "Isn't that sweet, Kristine?"

It was a picture of Anna, Kate, and the pup. The three of them were all snuggled together in the bed, sound asleep and peaceful as could be. The next picture was the same thing, only Anna had rolled over. She and the mutt were lying so close, their noses almost touched. Then there was one of Mattie stretched out—flat on her back. All four legs were sprawled apart. It looked like one front paw was on Anna's cheek and her other was holding Kate's nose.

Daddy laughed at that one.

"They are sweet." He kissed Mama on the cheek. "We should have an 8 by 10 made. We could frame it and put it up on the mantel. What do you think, Kristine?"

I smiled. I nodded. I agreed with everything they said about how absolutely wonderful the pictures were.

But inside . . .

Between the thunderstorm, trying to sleep next to "Flopping Anna," and a puppy that vibrated like an overloaded washing machine on the spin cycle, I hardly got any sleep at all. Then I bummed out on my math test, got in trouble for talking in social studies, got ignored by Brandon Leonard, and . . .

Then I had to sit and ooh and aah over pictures that . . . that . . . I should have been in. Me! Sleeping all cozy and warm between Kate and Anna. Not that lazy dog.

Maybe that's why what happened *wasn't* an accident after all.

chapter 17

When we finished looking at the pictures, I got up to go make dinner. Mama followed me to the kitchen.

Once I found the green beans, I turned toward the electric can opener beside the fridge. Mama took the can from me. "I'll do that, hon. Go ahead and play with your puppy." Then over the hum of the can opener, she added, "It'll be a few minutes. You might as well feed her, while you're outside."

Glancing at the back door, I hesitated a moment. I wasn't in the mood to play with the puppy right now.

"Think I'll go put on my shorts first."

"Good idea," Mama called over her shoulder. "Can you believe how hot it was today?"

I changed out of my school clothes and put on my shorts. It made me feel better already.

For the longest time, I stood and stared into my closet. After flipping through my outfits, I finally picked out one of my nice "church" dresses and hung it on the door. When I stepped back and looked at it, it made me smile.

Maybe if I wore something nice tomorrow . . . maybe if I felt like I looked better . . . maybe I might actually feel better. It couldn't be any worse than today was!

I'd just gotten back to the kitchen when Kate started squalling. I stopped at the doorway.

"Want me to go get her for you?"

Mama shook her head. "No. Probably needs her diaper changed."

Kate let out another wail.

"Is she okay?"

"Think it's just colic," Mama said. "You and Anna both had it. Thing is, I don't remember either of you throwing up as much as Kate has. Why don't you go ahead and feed Mattie? Supper's almost ready. You can play with her later."

I stepped aside so Mama could get past, then headed for the door. Once I was outside, Mattie came tearing up. Wagging her tail and bouncing around, she slammed against my legs. The instant her sharp little claws hit my bare leg, I yelled and leaped aside. That made her even more excited. She hopped up at least three more times, scratching my legs to bits, before I could push her back.

It wasn't a kick, but it *was* a little harder push than normal.

"That hurt!" I snarled in my meanest voice, as I stomped toward the door.

Mattie stood, wagging her tail and her whole rear end, at the bottom of the steps. I never saw her coming.

This time those sharp claws of hers almost seemed to rip right into my skin. I jumped away from her, but that only made the pup more excited. Her sharp little puppy claws tore at my bare legs once more.

I ran for the door.

"Leave me alone! *Stop it!*"

The turkey bell jingled when I yanked the door open. It jingled again when I leaped inside and let it slam.

Mattie yelped. Somehow she was right under my feet. The turkey bell jingled when she pulled her leg free. She yelped again.

Only this time the yelp was higher—more like a shriek.

A chill shot up my back.

I opened the door and took a step toward her. Mattie cowed down. Head low, she looked up at me with big brown frightened eyes and whimpered again.

"Hush!" I said.

When she stepped away from me, she yelped.

Only this time, it wasn't a yelp or a shriek. It was a scream!

High-pitched, shrill piercing—it knifed through the hot, humid air.

Maybe if I picked her up she'd quit crying. When I stooped to reach out for her, the door slid off my hip. The turkey bell jingled when it slammed. Those frightened eyes seemed to cut into me like her scream had cut through the warm air. Holding one paw off the ground, she hopped away.

But she kind of lost her balance and had to put her paw down. Quickly, she yanked it up, started spinning in circles and . . . and . . . she screamed and cried and—she wouldn't stop.

chapter 18

Dr. Hale slipped the edge of the X ray under a couple of clips to hold it against the lighted bar.

"Clean break," he said, tapping it with his finger. "Won't be any problem. She'll heal just fine."

The picture of Mattie's leg looked huge. The light behind the X ray made the white line—the place where the break was between the two bones—look even bigger.

"We'll probably need to keep her overnight. Let the swelling go down. Sometime tomorrow afternoon I'll set it, put a cast on, and take another X ray to make sure we have it back together right." He reached over and ruffled my hair. "She'll be fine. You can probably come after her around five thirty or six."

"Do we need to keep her inside or try to keep her off the leg?" Mama asked.

Dr. Hale shook his head. "Nope. Just let her stay where she normally stays."

It was an accident! That's what I told everybody. That's what I told myself. It was the truth! It was an accident. I didn't mean to hurt her. All I wanted was to get away from those sharp claws that were ripping up my bare leg. It wasn't my fault.

Papa had the girls in the waiting room when we came out. He held Kate, draped over his shoulder. She was sound asleep. Anna was balanced on his right leg. Her head snapped up when we walked out. Then her bottom lip stuck out and she started crying.

"Mattie. Where's Mattie?" she whimpered.

There was a lady sitting across from them with a poodle. A man next to her with a bird dog. When Anna started crying, the two dogs started barking. When the two dogs started barking, the dogs in the kennel joined in.

When Dr. Hale heard all the commotion, he smiled and held up a finger. "Whoever was next, hang on a second."

"What's her name?" Dr. Hale asked Mama.

"Anna."

"Anna," he said. "Your puppy is just fine. Come on. I'll show you."

Papa, Daddy, and Anna followed the vet to the back of the clinic. They were gone a long time. When they came back, Anna was still sniffling. But at least she wasn't squalling and making all the dogs in the place bark.

On the ride home, Mama and Daddy said stuff like: "Accidents happen," and "It wasn't your fault," and "She'll be fine."

Papa never said a word.

Even wearing my pretty dress, school wasn't much better the next day. It wasn't a rotten day— just nothing spectacular. Mrs. McMasters took five of us aside and let us take the math quiz over again. This time I made a C on it. I passed Brandon in the hall, but he was busy scuffling with a couple of his friends and didn't notice me. I *sure* didn't say anything to him.

At lunch recess, everybody talked about what they were going to do over the weekend. I just listened. I never told anyone about the puppy—not even Selena.

At four thirty, Daddy and I drove into town to get Mattie. Dr. Hale's assistant, Emily, went to get her for us.

She was all smiles when she brought Mattie

from the kennels at the back. "This is the *sweetest* puppy I've ever seen," she cooed.

Mattie wagged her tail, wiggled, and tried to lick Emily in the face.

"She is a regular doll. I helped Dr. Hale set her leg. We have to put a muzzle on most dogs, but not this little girl. Never offered to bite or jump up and run away. Didn't even let out so much as a whimper. You've got yourself a real prize here, young lady."

She rubbed her cheek against Mattie's. The pup gave her a quick kiss, then Emily held her out for me.

"Here you go."

"Thank you." I smiled.

Mattie didn't try to lick me in the face. She didn't slurp my arm with her wet tongue. She didn't wiggle or wag her tail. Mattie just lay in my arms, very still.

Daddy stopped at the front desk for a second. I went on outside.

"I really am sorry, Mattie," I said, once the door closed behind me. "I didn't mean to hurt you."

Mattie lay in my arms with her head draped over my wrist.

"Honest. I didn't mean to let the door slam. I'm glad you're going to be okay."

She kept her head down. Perfectly still, the only things that moved were her eyes.

Daddy came out and we hopped into the car. I was very careful getting in, so I wouldn't bump Mattie's cast. I let her ride in my lap instead of putting her on the seat between us. She rested her head on my leg, but she didn't try to lick me. And she didn't wiggle.

When we stopped at the hardware store, Mattie raised her head to see where Daddy was going. He wasn't gone long. When he came out he laid a box between us on the seat. It was about a foot long, about three inches tall and three inches wide. I glanced at it, then at Daddy.

"Door-closer." He answered before I could ask. "If I'd remembered the darned thing, all this would never have happened. I'm sorry, Kristine. I'll fix it as soon as we get home."

When we got to the house, Mama opened the front door.

"How are you doing, sweetheart?"

Mama was glad to see her. Mattie was glad to see Mama.

Tail whipping back and forth, she raced to the steps. She didn't race very fast, because of the big chunk of plaster on her leg. When she got to the steps, she tripped and bumped her chin. Mama started after her, but Mattie hopped up and managed to get herself, and her cast, up the steps before Mama could reach her. The puppy was all wiggle and bounce. Mama could barely hold her.

After they said their hellos, Mama handed Mattie back to me and we went inside.

"Did the doctor give any special instructions, or tell us to be careful about certain things? Anything like that?"

"Didn't see him," Daddy answered. "The receptionist said we needed a dry place for Mattie to stay. You know, if it rains, try not to get the cast wet. Other than that—it's pretty much leave her alone and let her heal. He does want to see her again in about two weeks, though."

The minute we came through the door, Anna leaped up and raced over. Mama caught her and motioned me to the couch. We sat down and she showed Anna the cast, let her feel it, and talked to her about how she couldn't race around the backyard for a while. She explained that she had to be real careful with Mattie.

I finally let go of the pup because she was wiggling and scratching me, trying to get to Anna. Once Anna had her, she snuggled her—wiggles and all. She let Mattie lick her on the face. She even puckered her lips, kissing her back.

After a while Mama told me to put Mattie outside, then wash up for supper. While Daddy worked on installing the new door-closer, I set the pup on the ground and fixed her some fresh water in her drinking bowl. She sat—right where I put her.

"Come on. It's cold water. Come and get a drink."

She just sat there. Head down, she watched Daddy working on the door.

"I know you're thirsty," I urged. "Come on."

She glanced at me, with only the tops of her eyes. She didn't move. Daddy closed the door and I went to fix her food. I glanced over my shoulder at her. She must have been really thirsty, because now she was slurping and lapping the water like mad. She drank and drank and drank.

Daddy opened the door again and adjusted the little screw-thing on the end of the cylinder. I set the food bowl beside Mattie. Water still dripping from her chin, she shied away.

"I'm not going to hurt you." I smiled, trying to keep my voice soft and gentle. "It was an accident. Come on. Come get your food."

She stopped a few feet away. Daddy tested the

door again. Cowed down with her tail tucked and her head low, she watched me from the top of her eyes.

"I told you I was sorry. Come on. Come and eat."

Never lifting her head, but watching every move, Mattie just sat.

I turned and went inside.

chapter 19

On Monday, Daddy went back to work. I had to ride the bus.

Only I didn't get to visit with Selena, or see if Brandon Leonard would notice me, or even get pestered by Matt Green calling me "Curly Sue."

Bus 4 was the one that ran the route where we lived. Bus 7 was the one that went past Meme's house. When Mama and Daddy were both at work, Mama took me to school and I waited at Meme's until she came to pick me up. It had been so long since I'd ridden Bus 4, I didn't even know who was on it.

So I stood at the end of our driveway and waited. And waited. And waited.

I was just about to head back to the house to tell Mama that they'd forgotten me, when I spotted the yellow bus rumbling up our section line. The door swung open and Coach Moore smiled down at me.

"Sorry. Had bus trouble this morning." She glanced at her watch. "Should be here about twenty minutes earlier from now on. Find a seat. We're running late."

Coach Moore screeched to a stop behind the school. "Don't think the tardy bell's rung yet," she called. "Don't push getting off the bus, but hurry on into the building."

The playground was empty, except for one boy. I didn't pay any attention to who it was because of all the jostling and shoving and pushing, as people tried to get off the bus.

I didn't pay any attention until Matt Green was right in my face.

"Is Mattie okay? What happened to her?"

It took me by surprise. "Huh?"

"Mattie?" he repeated. "Is she all right?"

He was so close, I couldn't move. Some of the kids bumped me out of the way, trying to get around us. When we got shoved so much that we were pressed together, he took a step or two back. His face was a little red when he cleared his throat.

"Is Mattie okay?" he repeated.

"How did you know about . . ."

"My cousin, Emily, works for Dr. Hale." Matt shrugged. "Is Mattie all right? How did it happen?"

I kind of froze. Matt was in front of me again. Right in my face.

All I said was, "The dog's fine. I'm late for class."

Over the next couple of weeks, things finally started looking up some. Matt Green left me alone. A new girl, Bonnie Perkins, moved in. She was a fifth grader, so she came to our room. She rode Bus 4, so we sat together on the bus. Mama took Kate in for her first checkup and the doctor said she was doing fine, and not to worry about the colic, unless she started losing weight. I dug in and studied hard for the next math test. Managed to make a B+. We won our first softball scrimmage. I even got to start.

Well it was only because Robyn Jones had the flu and missed school. Coach Moore put me in right field. I was glad that nobody hit the ball that way. My second time at bat, I got a base hit.

The next morning, when we were changing classes, Brandon Leonard gave me a "thumbs-up" when we passed in the hall.

"Good hit yesterday, Kristine." He smiled.

Okay—things weren't just "looking up." Things were *great!*

On Saturday we drove Grandma and Grandpa Rankin to the airport. They were going to a place called Somerset in England. It's where Grandpa's great-grandfather lived before the family moved to America. Grandma and Grandpa were so excited, they acted like little kids.

On Monday we took Mattie to the vet. He checked the leg and took another X ray. He said her break was healing great. We didn't have to bring her back for three and a half weeks. That's when he'd take the cast off.

Everyone could tell Mattie was doing better. When Anna would come out in the backyard, the pup would tear around—wiggling and bouncing so much you could hardly tell she had a cast on. They ran and played with each other. Anna laughed and giggled. Mattie wagged and licked her all over.

During those two weeks, things got lots better.

But it wasn't until we got home from the vet's, that afternoon, that things really started to happen.

That was the first day—in my whole entire life—that I ever felt in control.

Before then, I just felt like any other little kid, I guess. My parents told me what to do at home.

Teachers bossed me around at school. Coach bossed us around on the field. Someone *else* made up all the rules. The best we could do was try to follow them and stay out of trouble. I never got to tell anyone what to do.

And this sudden sense of control and power came—almost like a gift—from the most unlikely of places.

chapter 20

For two weeks, Mattie had avoided me. When I came out to feed her, she limped away. Tail tucked and head bowed, she acted like I'd beaten her with a club. I never had to scold her for jumping on me or for scratching on the back door. She never got close.

In a way, it made life easier.

There were a couple of times—watching her play with Anna, or when Daddy brought her in to lie on the couch with him—that I couldn't help but smile and think how cute she was. A part of me yearned to play with her—to laugh at her antics—to hold her tight while she wiggled—to cuddle her gently while she dozed. I always managed to catch myself, though.

I was *not* going to be tempted. I would *not* let myself be drawn in. If I dropped my guard for so much as a minute . . .

No!

I'd already been through that. Dandy wasn't in the pasture where she belonged. She didn't whinny at me when I got off the bus. I couldn't tell her what happened at school, or that Brandon Leonard had noticed me, or that I got picked first for a softball game.

I was glad that Mattie stayed away from me. It made it easier *not* to care for her.

I guess—the day we came home from our second visit to the vet—Mattie forgot how dangerous I was.

When we got to the house, I put Mattie down so she could take care of business. She took a quick squat, then raced to the front door and started bouncing against the screen. Mama opened the door for her and she ran straight for Anna. They chased and wrestled around in the living room. Anna squealed as Mattie raced back and forth across the floor. (She tripped over her cast a couple of times, but that never slowed her down.) Mama finally took them outside, because Anna tripped over stuff, too—and she didn't even have on a cast. I think Mama was afraid she was going to end up bumping her head on the coffee table or the hearth. Outside they ran and chased. The two of them were all over the backyard. Both clumsy little kids, it didn't matter if they fell. There was nothing but grass to land on.

When Mama took Anna inside for her bath, I went to feed Mattie. I barely stepped out the door when she started jumping up on me. Now that the weather had cooled some, and was back like it was supposed to be for this time of year, her jumping didn't hurt. I had on my jeans. I didn't want to push her away, because she might hurt her leg again. So I just let her bounce against me while I fixed her fresh water, then picked up her food bowl.

We kept the dry dog food in a big can on the back porch. I filled the scoop and dumped it in Mattie's bowl. Suddenly I noticed there was nothing hitting my leg.

Mattie was gone!

I glanced around to see what happened to her. Mama stood just outside the back door. She held Anna—wrapped in a towel after her bath—in one arm. With her free hand, she was trying to undo the little turkey bell from the back door.

I guess I expected to see Mattie bouncing against her leg, trying to get at Anna. Only Mattie wasn't there, either. I finally spotted her. She was about ten feet away—head down, eyes wide, and tail tucked, she watched Mama. She didn't wiggle. She didn't wag her tail. She just watched.

Mama switched arms and used her right hand to try to untie the little bell. Anna scrunched her neck down against Mama's shoulder.

"Cold!" she complained.

Mama gave up on the bell and motioned to me. "When you get through feeding Mattie, bring this bell inside. We need to take it back to Meme C, the next time we go."

I nodded. Mama stepped inside and started drying Anna. I brought the food bowl back, and all of a sudden, little paws hit my jeans. Mattie was here again. Little tail whipped the air. Little ears bounced with excitement.

"Quit that," I scolded.

She just wiggled and bounced some more. I set the food bowl beside the back door and reached for the string that held the turkey bell. Again, she scampered away to huddle close to the ground. As soon as I let go of the bell and walked toward her, she came to me again.

"Quit jumping!" I scolded.

She didn't.

I walked to the back door and shook the little turkey bell. All fours hit the ground, and Mattie scampered out into the yard. With a smile, I untied the turkey bell from the back door. But I didn't take it inside to Mama. I put it in my pocket.

The puppy learned quick. After the second day, all I had to do was shout an order at her and reach for the bell. It wasn't long before a simple snap of my fingers, a mean look, or speaking in a firm tone stopped her from bouncing against my leg.

It was a little funny. A little strange, too.

I tried to be a nice kid. That's what Mama and Daddy said. I was quiet and made sure to stay out of trouble. I didn't call people names or bully them. I was scared of a lot of things. Spiders. Wasps. Afraid of being embarrassed by getting my name put on the board for talking in class. Afraid of getting sent to the office. Afraid of getting in trouble with Mama or Daddy.

But no one—not one single person or thing on the face of this earth—had ever been afraid of *me*.

Now, it was different.

All I had to do was pull the turkey bell from my pocket, and Mattie would stop what she was doing—race to hunker down in the yard, all shaky and trembly.

Now I wanted to train her to come to me, too.

That took more work than getting her to scamper off.

If I held my hands out—showed her they were empty—then dropped down on my knees and patted my legs, she would come closer. And if I held my hand out, called to her in my sweetest voice, and smiled—she would ease near enough for me to pet her. It took almost an entire week of coaxing and sweet-talking to get her to do that.

But it was just in time.

"Papa and Meme are coming over after church Sunday, for dinner," Mama announced when we finished supper on Friday and headed for the TV room. "Any ideas what to fix?"

"I haven't cranked up the smoker for a while," Daddy said. "How about a hickory-smoked brisket?"

"Cake," Anna said, droozling milk down her chin.

"You could fix that rice and broccoli casserole, Lauren." Daddy licked his lips.

"Yeah," I added. "Lots of cheese and pecans on top." I licked my lips, too.

"Cake," Anna said again.

"Think we should have a salad or something? To go along with it?" Mama peeked into the freezer to make sure she had a sack of frozen broccoli.

"Might as well," Daddy said.

"Cake!" Anna yelled.

We all turned to look at her. How she got her knees out from under the lid of her high chair so she could stand up, I have no idea. But there she was—fists on her hips—standing on the seat, as the tall chair wobbled back and forth.

"Cake!"

Mama snatched Anna up, before she turned the chair over, and snuggled her tight. Daddy rolled his eyes.

"Good catch," he told Mama. "Just what kind of cake would you like, young lady?"

"Cake."

"How about that German Chocolate Cake?" I suggested. "You know, the one with coconut and pecan icing . . ."

"Yeah, lots of extra icing," Daddy added.

"Do you know how long it takes to make that icing?"

"Cake!" Anna squawked.

Mama looked at her and let out a little chuckle.

"Cake it is. German Chocolate Cake, with plenty of extra icing."

chapter 21

"Best cake I ever ate." Papa rocked back in the recliner and patted his tummy. "Catherine, I do believe your daughter's got you beat when it comes to German Chocolate Cake." Then real soft, he added, "Think I might sneak back in the kitchen and have me another piece."

"You will do no such thing." Meme popped her dish towel at him from where she stood in the doorway to the kitchen. "You've already had two pieces. You're not supposed to be eating smoked meat, either, and you scarfed that brisket down like you were starving to death. That's enough."

Papa patted his tummy again. "Grumpy old woman," he mumbled to Daddy. "Got ears like a bat."

"I heard that!" Meme called from the kitchen.

"Need some help with the dishes?" I asked Mama and Meme.

"We're fine, Kristine," Mama answered. "Almost got them done. Are the boys watching a football game?"

"It's not football season," I answered. "Basketball."

Meme shrugged. "Whatever."

I eased out the back door and went to find Mattie.

She stood beside the little plastic doghouse that Daddy had bought for her. She wagged her tail and watched. Kneeling down in the middle of the backyard, I patted my legs. She bounded toward me. Just before she got in "leaping" range—almost close enough to start hopping on me—I snapped one hand up, and reached for my pocket with the other.

She slid to a halt.

"Sit," I ordered.

Still wagging her tail, wiggling all over, and wanting to come to me, Mattie crouched, but she didn't sit.

"Sit," I repeated.

Her ears flattened and she sat down. I made her stay there for about ten seconds, before I dropped my hand and patted my leg. "Come on, Mattie. Come on, pup." She scampered to my side, almost wagging herself to pieces while I petted her back and stroked her head.

After a few seconds, I eased to my feet. Mattie's ears flattened and her tail tucked as she scooted away from me. I patted my leg once more.

"Come on, sweetheart." I made my voice sugary. She moved a step or two closer. "That's my sweet little dog."

She came back to my side. She didn't jump against my leg, though. Head low and watching my every move out of the tops of her eyes, she followed a step or two behind as I walked to the far corner of the yard. I circled around the lilac bush. When I stopped, she stopped. When I walked, she followed.

"Sit."

Ears flat and tail tight against her rump, Mattie sat.

"Stay." I held my palm out at her and backed away. She started to get up, once. I touched my pocket. She froze like a Popsicle. I left her that way for a few seconds, then dropped to my knees and patted my leg. Tongue flopping and tail spinning behind her like a helicopter, she raced to me.

It was time.

I suggested everyone come to the backyard, so I could show them how well I had trained Mattie.

I could hardly wait.

When everyone came piling through the back door and onto the porch, Mattie went wild. She raced to us, leaping and wiggling. I snapped my fingers and held my hand up to stop her, but she didn't even notice. She pounced against Anna, almost knocking her down. She hopped against Papa's leg. He laughed and reached down to pet her. She raced to Meme before he even bent over. I yelled her name, once. Her ears flattened and her head ducked—but for only an instant. Then she bounded off again.

Anna squealed and galloped around the yard with Mattie hot on her heels. Then she turned and chased Mattie. Everyone said how cute they were.

"What did you want to show us?" Meme asked, finally.

My head drooped so low, my chin almost rested against my chest. "Nothing."

"There are too many people and too much excitement. Why don't we go inside and watch from the kitchen?" Mama suggested. "You think that would help, Kristine?"

With a nod, I smiled at her.

It took a moment or two to round everybody up—especially Anna. But once inside the house, Mattie still wouldn't do what she was supposed to.

She kept trying to get them to come back outside and play with her.

"Mattie," I called.

She ignored me.

"Come on, Mattie. Let's show them how smart you are."

Her tail was wagging so hard, it's a wonder it didn't knock her feet out from under her.

"**MATTIE!**" I roared her name, and yanked the bell from my pocket.

Instantly she dropped. Spinning around to face me, her ears flattened and her head ducked. Tail tucked under her tummy, she made a wide arch around me as she raced for her doghouse at the far corner of the yard.

Replacing the turkey bell, I slowly dropped to my knees in the middle of the yard. Patted my legs.

"Come here, Mattie," I cooed. "Come here, you little sweet puppy."

Her ears perked. She took only one step toward me, then stopped and cowered against the side of the doghouse.

"Come on, honey. That's a good little girl. Come to me."

Mattie sprang forward, bounding across the yard with her tail spinning behind her. When she got close enough, I held up my hand. She slid to a stop.

"Sit." I commanded.

She sat. I patted my legs again and she came to me. I petted her and let her wiggle and jump against me. I even let her lick me in the face with that floppy wet tongue of hers. Then I eased to my feet. "Come." She followed. Walked when I walked. Stopped when I stopped.

It worked like a dream. She did everything— *exactly* like we had practiced. I could hardly wait to get back in the house so Meme and Papa could tell me what a wonderful job I had done, training her.

There was no one in the kitchen when I opened the door. Frowning and puzzled, I started through the house to see where everyone went.

They weren't in the living room, either. The front door opened, and Mama came in, holding Kate in her arms. Through the doorway, I could see Daddy and Anna on the front porch.

"Where are Meme and Papa? Did they leave?"

Mama nodded.

"Why? What's wrong, is Papa sick?"

Frowning, Mama shook her head. "I don't think so. He seemed to be feeling okay. He just thanked us for the meal and said, 'It's time to go home.'"

"But why? What happened?"

Mama gave a helpless shrug. "No idea."

"I'll go find out."

"Kristine, your Papa's in one of his 'moods.' Just leave him alone."

I ignored her, sidestepped to get around, and headed for the door.

"Kristine," Mama called from behind me.

I didn't slow down—not one little bit. This wasn't right! This wasn't the way it was supposed to be. Papa didn't say a single word about how well I had trained Mattie. He didn't say how sweet we looked, playing together. How—even as young as she was—she already knew how to sit, follow me, and come when she was called.

Daddy stood outside on the porch, holding Anna's hand. They both waved at the old pickup that was backing out of our driveway. I darted past them, leaped down the steps, and raced across the yard.

Meme didn't see me coming because she was turned around, looking over her shoulder while she backed. She didn't hear me, either, because the window was up.

I rapped on the glass with my knuckles. A bit startled, she whipped her head around. When she saw me standing there, she rolled down the window.

"Why did you leave?" I demanded.

"We need to get home." She smiled. "Chores and things need to be taken care of. And . . . ah . . . and it's getting late."

Meme could always tell when I was lying. This time I could tell she was lying.

"Why did you leave?" I repeated.

On the other side of the truck, Papa's door flew opened. He got out and slammed it so hard, the whole truck shook.

"You want to know why?" He growled, stomping around the truck toward me. "You really want to know why?"

"Yes," I growled back.

"Fine! I'll tell you why!"

I wished I'd listened to Mama.

chapter 22

"There's a big difference between training a puppy and having a poor dog who's so terrified she trembles at the mere sight of you."

Despite the strain on my neck to stare straight up at him, I felt my mouth flop open. "What?"

"Mattie! She's scared to death of you!"

"But she comes when I call her. I pet her and all that sort of stuff."

"Yeah!" Papa snapped, taking another step toward me. "But it's not because you love her, or because she's trying to please you. It's because she's afraid *not* to mind you!

"What did you do, hit her? Whack her with a switch? Threaten to break her other leg?"

Meme's door opened. "*Larry!* That's enough."

"It was an accident, Papa. I didn't mean to hurt

her. I feed her and give her fresh water, every day. Mama never has to do that stuff. I do it all. And—and—"

He took another step. I had to back up again.

Suddenly he knelt in front of me and took hold of my shoulders.

"Kristine, have you ever loved her?"

The knot stuck in my throat. I couldn't even swallow. He gave me a little shake—not hard enough to hurt, but enough to make me look at him. **"Have you?"**

Papa's voice was an angry growl. Mean. Frightening. I'd never seen Papa mad before. It scared me. Finally I looked at him. But out of the corner of my eye, I could see Meme. She stood next to us. Reaching out, she took his arm.

"Larry. Calm down. You're getting yourself all upset. You know what the doctors said. Let's just get in the car. You and Kristine can talk some other time—when you're calmer."

"No, Catherine!" He snapped, jerking his elbow loose from her grasp. "This is important. It needs to be done—*NOW!*"

"I didn't want her at first, but—but I didn't want to hurt your feelings . . . and . . . then . . . I love her, now?"

I heard my voice go up on the end of what I said. Even to me, it sounded more like a question. I just hoped Papa hadn't noticed.

He sighed, but his eyes never left mine.

"Do you love her as much as you did Dandy?"

I didn't answer. I couldn't.

"You can't love her because you're afraid of her."

"Huh?"

"You're ten times more scared of that sweet little puppy, than she could ever be of you."

Now I took a step forward. Bumped *his* little, round tummy with *my* chest. Papa took a step back. Chin jutting out, I glared up at him.

"She's just a puppy. I'm not afraid of some dumb, little-ole puppy!"

"Yes you are, Kristine. You're scared to death of her." He peeked down at me, then quickly closed his eyes once more. "You're afraid that if you love her— then if something happens to her—it will hurt."

I couldn't argue about that. But Papa just didn't understand.

"You care more about that little dog than you do about me," I snapped at him. "Don't you, Papa?"

With a sigh, he leaned to rest against the pickup.

"This isn't about the dog, Kristine. It's about you."

"What do you mean, it's about *me?*"

My words were strangely soft—almost a whisper.

Taking a couple of deep breaths, nearly panting, Papa just shook his head. "Every living thing, born on the face of this earth, will die.

"That's just the way life is. We all know the ending. There's no way to change it. Nothing we can do to prevent it. It just *is*.

"You can't spend your life worrying about the hurt that *might* come. You have to learn to enjoy the wonderful things around you. Dandy was a good old horse. Don't be mad at God for taking her away. Don't hate that puppy, just so you won't have to hurt when she goes. Do you understand, Kristine?"

I tried to smile. "I understand, Papa," I lied. "I'm sorry."

"Please don't be scared of that little puppy. Don't be afraid of me."

"Afraid of you?" I frowned up at him. "Just what is that supposed to mean?"

Papa sighed and shook his head. He threw his hands up in surrender.

"I'm fifty-eight years old. I never took very good care of myself, and with all the smoking I did, I've been living on borrowed time for years. More than likely, I'll be the next to go."

"But Papa—"

"Larry, don't say things like that to her." Meme rushed over, trying to get between us.

Turning away from both of us, Papa opened the passenger-side door. He had to bounce a couple of times before he could swing into the cab and sit down.

"But, Papa . . ."

He closed the door and sat staring out the window. When I moved to the front of the pickup, he turned his eyes to look out the side glass.

"Wait here for just a second," I said between gritted teeth. "Okay?"

Without another word, I stormed off toward the house and got the dog.

"Here!" I said, stuffing Mattie into Meme's arms. "Since I don't know how to love her, or how to treat her, she'll be better off with *him!*"

I guess I expected Meme to argue with me—to try and talk me into keeping Mattie. She just took her, got into the pickup, and closed the door. Mattie bounded across the front seat. She leaped against Papa and started licking his face.

He patted her, but he didn't look at her. He didn't look at me, either. He just let her hop against his chest and lick him.

Mama and Daddy stood watching with the little kids at the front door. Crying and whimpering, Anna held her arms out toward the pickup. When I burst through, Daddy swooped her up in his arms so I wouldn't run over her. Once they were out of my way, I raced to my room and slammed the door behind me.

chapter 23

When I was a little kid, I spent a lot of time hiding under my bed. If I wanted something, and didn't get my way—I crawled under my bed and pouted. If I got in trouble with Mama or Daddy for doing something I shouldn't—I hid under my bed. Sometimes, when I was just feeling sad or blue or lonely—I would lie there and think about how things would be when I was big and all grown up.

But I *did* grow up. I *was* bigger. Older. I was eleven and had left those childish things behind, a long, long time ago.

It is a little dusty under here, I thought. *Next time we clean my room so Mama can sweep, I need to remind her to vacuum under my bed.*

When I wiped my eyes, they still stung a little.

Guess it was from grinding the salty tears in with the back of my hands.

I'd cried for a while but not very long. Mostly I was mad at Papa for saying all those things to me. He was just mean. All he was trying to do was hurt my feelings because of that stupid dog.

"Kristine?" Mama called from the hallway. "Meme C is on the phone."

I scooted from under the bed, so my voice wouldn't be muffled by the mattress and all the boxes that were stored there.

"I'm doing my homework." I forced my voice to be light and cheerful. "Is it okay if I call her later?"

"Are you all right?"

"I'm fine. Honest." I sounded so bright and shiny, I almost believed me, myself. "Just not at a good place to stop, right now. Need to finish this chapter. Okay?"

"I'll let her know you'll call later." The way Mama's voice faded, I could tell she was heading back to the living room.

I crawled back under the bed. "Just a dumb dog," I snorted. When I breathed out, a few of the little dust particles spun and swirled into the air. The light that crept through my west window caught them. They seemed to sparkle and dance as they drifted back down.

Only she wasn't a dumb dog. She was a puppy. Playful, wiggly, full of bounce and licks and energy. All she wanted to do was give me little puppy kisses with her tongue or get me to pet her.

"Kristine?" The sound of Mama's voice at my bedroom door startled me. I rose up so quickly that I clunked my head on the box springs.

Quick as a cat, I scooted from under the bed.

"Yes?" I called back—all bright and cheery.

There was a long pause from the other side of the door. "Are you okay?"

"I'm fine, Mama. I really need to finish this chapter."

Back under my bed, when I closed my eyes, I could almost see that night at Eduardo's. Papa had been so proud and happy that his wrinkly old face seemed to glow. Mattie came flying out of that box, wagging her tail so hard and wiggling so much that her rump almost bumped into her nose. When I tucked her inside my jacket so we could sneak through the kitchen, she chewed on my thumb and fingers. Those sharp little puppy teeth almost hurt. She licked awhile, wiggled, and started gnawing again. When we got back to my birthday party and I opened my coat, she almost knocked herself apart, trying to crawl up and kiss my face and . . .

And . . . I shoved her at Selena and wouldn't even pet her.

Watching her race around in the grass at the hospital parking lot took my mind off Mama. For just a moment I forgot how scared I was. I forgot about how dangerous and uncertain having a baby can be. I forgot how fragile a newborn is. For a moment Mattie made me forget to worry about Mama. And made me smile. As I'd watched her, I saw how new and exciting and fun life really was, and . . .

I opened my eyes because the thought . . . the memory . . . the feelings that came made me want to cry again. I felt like my insides were being torn apart. Like there were two strings on my heart, pulling and stretching in opposite directions. I could hear the pounding in my ears. Feel it thumping in my throat. The mad pulled me one way. The joy from remembering Mattie's little puppy antics pulled me the other way, and . . . and . . .

I wouldn't cry!

I didn't cry.

I forced myself to stare down at the floor. I forced myself—worked as hard as I could—to chase the feelings away.

Dandy was gone. Now, Mattie was gone. Maybe

she would be better off with Meme and Papa. Maybe they could love her and play with her.

"Enough of this!" I snorted. Dust puffed into the air again. "You're eleven years old. You're too big to be hiding under your bed. You're too grown-up to lie around and feel sorry for yourself. You can't spend your whole life thinking about some dumb old horse. Enough is enough. Besides, as dusty as it is under here, if you stay much longer, you'll probably make yourself sick. Mattie's better off with Meme and Papa. Maybe I'm better off, too."

Two weeks later, I *still* didn't feel better off.

And . . .

there was *still* dust under my bed.

It was all on account of that dumb little Anna. Well . . . her and Selena. Both of them were such a pain.

The morning after Papa's big blowup, Anna had stood at the back door in her pajamas. "I want to go play with Mattie." When Mama reminded her that Mattie wasn't there, she boohooed. It was the same the next morning. Then she forgot about it for a while. But when the weekend came, she whined and bawled and sniffed again.

Selena had caught me on the way to the buses

after school on that next day. She'd asked if I could come over to her house for the afternoon.

"We could fix our hair," she suggested. "Or we could talk about boys or just watch TV or—"

"I'd love to, Selena," I said, cutting her off. "But I've got to study."

Selena thrust her arm through the strap on her backpack and slung it over her shoulder. With her hands free, she jabbed both fists on her hips and glared at me.

"Look, Kristine. We're both in the same room. We both have the same classes and the same subjects. There are no tests tomorrow. No test for the rest of the week, for that matter. Just what is it that you need to study?"

My shoulders sagged when I sighed. "Social studies. I bombed on the test today. Made a forty-five on it. Mrs. McMasters told me she'd let me take it over again tomorrow."

The look on Selena's face was almost scary.

"Social studies? *Social studies?* When I called last night, your mom told me you couldn't come to the phone, because you were studying for your social studies test." Selena looked like she was totally lost. "What did you do, study the wrong chapter?"

"I—er—I—ahhhh . . ." All I could do was stammer.

Her upper lip curled to a sneer. "I don't know what I did to make you mad," she snapped. "I don't know what happened to make you not want to be my friend anymore. And you know something else?" She didn't give me time to answer before she said, "I. Don't. Care!"

"But Selena . . ."

"Forget it, Kristine! Every time I ask you to do something with me, you have to study. Every time I want to talk, you have to study. If you studied half as much as you claim, you'd be making straight A's. Just forget it! You don't want anything to do with me. I don't want anything to do with you."

With that, she spun toward the bus. Little whiffs of dirt puffed from beneath her feet as she stormed off.

I wanted to tell her about Papa, and the puppy, and all that had happened. I wanted to confess about acting like a little kid and hiding under my bed, crying, instead of studying like I told everyone I was doing. Only, all I did was stand there with my head hung low and watch her go.

A sound behind me snapped my head up. I glanced over my shoulder. Matt Green and Darrell

Porter charged straight toward me. Running as hard as they could, neither so much as acted like they were going to try and miss me. Muscles tensed, I braced myself for the impact.

At the last second, Darrell dodged to my right. His backpack brushed my arm. It didn't hurt, but he was running so fast that it hit me with enough force to kind of spin me around. Matt shot past on my other side. Gravel ground beneath his feet when he tried to stop. He slid about three or four yards past me. He turned around and kind of tilted his head far to the side.

"Hey, Curley . . . er . . . I mean Kristine. Is something wrong?"

"No. Just almost got run down by a couple of idiots." I shot him a look. "Why?"

He gave a little shrug. "Well, the look on your face . . . you . . . ah . . . you seem kind of sad or something."

"I'm just fine," I snipped. "What's it to you, anyway?"

Matt gave another little shrug.

"Absolutely nothing! You just looked like you lost your best friend, or . . . somebody tinkled on your toothbrush. Judging by the attitude, I guess it was your toothbrush."

I went home on Bus 4. It was a pretty day, and

Anna was outside. She wondered around the backyard, looking behind the shrubs, peeking in the doghouse, and pouting.

I managed a B+ on my social studies makeup test. After a couple of days, I figured Selena had had enough time to cool off. I spotted her in the lunchroom and took my tray to set it across from her. She glanced up when I smiled and sat down. Then she stuffed a spoonful of apple crisp in her mouth, got up, and left for recess.

Yesterday I'd asked her if she wanted to come over and spend the weekend.

"Sorry. I've got to wash my hair."

When I got home, Anna was standing at the back door. There were nose spots on the glass, where she'd stood and stared longingly into the yard. And her eyes were red.

Like I said, there was still dust under my bed.

chapter 24

"Find anything interesting under there?"

The sound of Mama's voice startled me. When I jerked, my head bumped the box springs. Slithering from beneath the bed, I looked to see her kneeling in the open doorway to my room.

"What?" I asked, rubbing the sore spot on my head.

Mama nodded toward the bed. "Anything interesting under there?"

"Just dust."

"I'll clean house Monday." Mama smiled. "Get ready a little early for school, and we'll stack the boxes in the corner. I'll help you lean your mattress against the wall, so I can sweep. Think you can handle that?"

"I'll set my alarm up fifteen minutes."

Mama nodded. I was glad she didn't ask me

what I was doing under the bed. "I got breakfast cooking, and Kate just threw up again. You want to flip the pancakes and stir the scrambled eggs, or clean up the—"

"Eggs!" I answered before she could even finish.

After breakfast Mama did the dishes while I held Kate. She was fun to hold. Sometimes she wiggled and made weird faces. Her eyes were always moving. Jerking. Darting side to side, constantly exploring and curious. She squirmed and wiggled. And on occasions, funny little moans or squeaks came.

I loved it when her tiny fingers would wrap around one of mine. Meme had commented about how long and slender my fingers were. "You could make a great pianist one of these days, with those delicate hands," she'd said. But with Kate's fingers wrapped around one of mine, my hands looked *anything but* delicate. They looked fat and rough and big.

Daddy got home a little before noon. He gave Mama a little kiss. "You want to grab the kids and go to Jake's for barbecue, or get a take-out order and go see your folks?"

We spent the whole day with Papa and Meme C. Anna went straight outside the second we got there. She and Mattie chased around the yard. Anna squealed. Mattie barked. And they both ran and ran, until Daddy finally had to go get Anna and practically drag her inside for dinner. Papa was in a good mood. Even when Meme scolded him, because he tried to go back for a third helping of barbecue, he didn't get upset or fuss with her. After dinner we sat around and watched TV. Mama and Meme visited while Daddy and Papa took a nap. Kate slept in her carrier and Anna, who was worn out from all the running and squealing she did before dinner, curled up next to Daddy on the couch. When Papa started snoring, and Meme and Mama were sure everyone was settled and quiet, they sneaked off to the back bedroom. I watched TV for a few more minutes, then slipped off to see what they were up to. I found them digging around in a box of Mama's old clothes. When they finished, we went back to check on baby Kate.

Papa wasn't in the living room. When Meme spotted him sneaking another barbecue sandwich from the kitchen, I knew she was going to scold him about it.

I couldn't help but wonder why Meme usually fussed at Papa about what he ate. It wasn't like he was fat or anything. I mean . . . all the farmwork he did, he looked like he was in pretty good shape— for an old guy. Whenever I asked her, all she ever said was that he needed to watch his diet. I could never get her to tell anything more.

I don't know why grown-ups do that. Us kids can tell when there's something wrong, but they won't tell us what it is. Guess they don't want to worry us. But when you know something's not quite right, and nobody will tell you . . . well . . . it worries us more than knowing.

So I didn't bother to ask again. And . . .

It kind of surprised me when Meme didn't scold Papa, either. She just pretended she didn't see him and sat down to watch TV.

"Got to go move a couple of round bales for the cows," Papa announced when he came back from the kitchen. "Anybody want to go with me?"

He was looking straight at me. I noticed a little barbecue sauce at the corner of his mouth. Catching his eye, I dabbed at the corner of my mouth to warn him. He turned his head, so Meme couldn't see, wiped the sauce off, then gave me a quick wink when he turned back.

"Want to drive the tractor, Kristine?"

Papa hadn't said one single word about the dog. Even so, I had the feeling that once we got on the tractor, I was gonna get another lecture.

A bit reluctant, I managed to stand up and smile at him.

"Sure. I'll go."

* * *

All the time we were gone, not one single word was said about Mattie. Papa talked about his cows and about the weather—and then he began telling stories.

"There was this one time when your Meme and I went parking, out by Lake—" He stopped and cleared his throat. "Well . . . that story probably needs to wait until you're a little older." He cleared his throat again.

"You and Meme went parking?" I yelped.

He didn't answer.

"Papa?"

Still nothing.

"Ah, come on, Papa. Which lake was it, and what did you do, and . . ."

"You just watch where you're driving, Squirt. Your Meme would skin me alive if she found out I'd told a ten-year-old about—"

"I'm eleven, Papa," I protested.

"Ten. Eleven. Don't matter. Remind me again when you're twenty and I'll tell you all about it."

I glanced over my shoulder. When I was little, Papa used to let me sit in his lap and play like I was driving the tractor. When I got older, he even let me steer. Last year, when I was ten, he started letting me drive. He stood behind, holding on to the spring seat.

When I glanced around, I couldn't help but giggle about how red his face was. His cheeks turned an even brighter shade of pink when he saw me looking.

"Knock it off, Squirt," he growled. "Just shut up and drive."

Once the tractor was parked by the barn and I had the motor shut off, I leaped down from the seat and sprinted for the house.

"Don't you dare, Kristine," I heard Papa threaten as he chased after me. "You say one word to your Meme, and so help me . . ."

His threat was drowned out by Mattie's barking and the sound of my own laughter.

Meme stood, facing the front door. When Papa came in, she had her feet apart and both fists planted firmly against her hips.

"I cannot believe that you told this *child* about us going parking at Lake Lawtonka, Larry Wilson."

"I didn't tell her a thing," he panted. "She's just trying to get you to tell . . . her . . . Don't fall . . . for . . . it . . . and . . ."

Papa was breathing so hard, he could barely talk. The glare on Meme's face suddenly changed. She looked worried and scared.

"Larry? What is it? What's wrong?"

Papa reached for his chest. He only touched it a

second, then quickly slid his hand down to hold his stomach.

"Too . . . much . . . barbecue," he gasped.

Meme rushed to him. Holding his arm, she tried to help him to his chair. Papa wiggled his arm free. He struggled for a deep breath.

"I'm fine . . . ," he wheezed, "just ate too much. Then *ran* from . . . the barn, clean . . . to the . . . front door. A little winded . . . , that's all."

Mama and Daddy rushed to him, too. They tried to get him to sit down, but Papa refused.

I didn't notice the shaking before. Now I did! My hands trembled. My knees shook so hard I could barely stand. I had never been so scared in my whole entire life.

There was something wrong with Papa. Something serious!

And it was all my fault. If I hadn't teased him . . . if he hadn't chased me from the barn to the house . . .

It was all my fault!

chapter 25

Papa's shoulders sagged. But it wasn't like he was getting ready to collapse or pass out. It was more like he surrendered.

Still panting and wheezing, he let them lead him to his recliner. Meme raced to the kitchen to get him a glass of water. With one hand, Daddy pulled the lever to raise the footrest. With the other, he pushed the top of the recliner so far back, Papa was almost lying down. Mama snatched a magazine from the end table and started fanning him.

I just stood in the middle of the living room and shook.

Meme brought the water. Perfectly still, as if holding her breath, she watched until he'd taken a drink. "I think I need to call Dr. Paulson."

Papa licked his lips and shot her a disgusted look.

"Just give me a minute."

Daddy adjusted the footrest on the recliner. Meme shook her head. "Larry, you just came from the barn to the front door. It's not that far. You shouldn't be breathing so—"

He set the water glass down on the end table with a loud clunk.

"Old woman . . . I didn't walk from . . . the barn to the house." His chest filled with air. "I ran." He sucked in another quick breath and shook his head. "No, I didn't run. It was a . . . sprint. Now just give me a couple of minutes. I'm fine."

Daddy raised the back of Papa's recliner a little. Mama kept fanning. Although there was only a sip or two gone from the water glass, Meme grabbed it to fill it up again. I shook. Daddy lowered Papa's footrest a couple of notches, then raised it one click. Meme came back with the fresh glass of water and handed it to Papa. Daddy frowned, studying the position of the recliner, and took a step toward it while Mama kept fanning with the magazine.

Papa raised both hands, then straightened his arms as if shoving them back.

"Stop! All of you."

Frowning and worried, everyone stopped and watched him. Papa smiled.

"Lauren. You keep fanning me, I'm gonna catch pneumonia. Catherine. You pour any more water down me, I'm gonna be up all night running to the bathroom. And Richard. You adjust my chair—one more time—so help me, I'm gonna kick you right in the teeth."

It took a few minutes for his breathing to get back to normal. He kept glancing up at Meme and Mama and shaking his head. When Kate started crying in the other room, Mama left to go clean her up. Papa smiled. Then he squinted at Meme.

"Has anyone checked on Anna lately?"

Meme walked toward the back door, and Papa's smile got even bigger.

I was feeling better, too. My knees had stopped shaking, and there was only a little tremble left in my fingers.

But when Papa looked straight at me and frowned, I could feel my bottom lip start to bounce.

"Why the long face, Squirt?"

It was all I could do to keep from crying. A sly grin curled Papa's lips.

"I ever tell you the one about the horse who walked into the bar, and the bartender looked up and said, 'Why the long face?'"

He paused—waiting for me to laugh—or for me

to say, "I got it." All I could do was bite down on my bottom lip to keep it from flopping around.

That was one of Papa's favorite jokes. When I was little, I used to tell him knock-knock jokes. He'd let me tell about two or three, then he'd spring that one on me. I used to wait for the rest of the joke. It never came. I was probably about ten before I figured out what was so funny about the bartender asking a *horse,* about his *long* face.

When I clamped my lips together, a little squeak came out. Then the tears started. I raced to him. Practically threw myself, to wrap my arms around him and hug him as hard as I could.

"I didn't mean to hurt you," I bawled. "I'm sorry. I love you. I'm sorry. I'm so sorry . . ."

He hugged me back.

"I love you, too, Kristine. Always will."

We didn't lay there long before he kind of laughed and shoved me off his chest. "You're gonna flip us over, you keep wallerin' around on me like that. What are you bawlin' about. I'm fine. And why do you keep sayin' you're sorry. Sorry for what?"

"I didn't mean to hurt you, Papa."

"What's this 'hurt me' stuff? I ain't hurt. I'm just fine."

"But—but—" I sniffed. "I made you run . . . you know, chasing me. I didn't mean to—"

"Kristine." He squeezed my shoulders so tight, it almost hurt. "You're a very bright young lady. But that is the *dumbest* thing I ever heard! You didn't hurt me. I ate too much. I haven't run or jogged for years. I haven't even hauled hay since I got the new round baler. The only exercise I get is sitting on the tractor and riding around. I ate too much and I'm out of shape. I just got a little winded."

"But, Papa, you were trying to keep me from telling Meme—"

"I was teasing with you," he snapped, cutting me off. "I knew good and well your grandmother wasn't going to tell you anything she didn't figure you were old enough to hear, and . . ." He smiled at me. "I knew she was going to get on to me about talking about it. Got to get a rise out of the old woman sometimes. If she ain't fussing at me, I figure she don't love me.

"It was all my doing, Kristine. You had nothing to do with it. Fact is, the only way you could have prevented it was to take my barbecue sandwich away— and I would have fought you for it. Been a long time since I've had barbecue. Besides, I'm just fine."

I sniffed again. He pulled me so my head could rest on his shoulder.

"Better knock it off, or I'll grab me a switch and go chase you around the house."

I tried to laugh, only I couldn't. So I sniffed again.

"I ever tell you the one about the horse who walked into . . ."

"Oh, please don't tell that one again, Papa. I'll quit crying. I promise."

It was after dark when we finally went home. Once I had Mama and Daddy trapped in the car, I decided it was time to *make them* tell me what was wrong with Papa. When I first asked, they just told me he ate too much and was out of shape. The same thing Papa told me.

"No!" I leaned over the front seat, as far as I could, so I could look Mama square in the face. "You and Meme both keep fussing at him about what he eats. Every time he comes in from the field, Meme watches him like a hawk, until she's sure he is all right. Something is wrong with him, and I want to know *what!* Right now!"

Mama's head kind of snapped back, a little startled that I was shouting at her. Her eyes tightened, giving me one of her stern looks. I just leaned farther. Got my face right in hers.

"Grown-ups don't want kids to worry about stuff. But I know something's wrong. Don't you get it? Even if I *am* a kid, it's more scary *not* to know what's going on. Please?"

Mama glared at me for only a second. Then with a sigh, she let her shoulders sag. Careful not to bump Kate's car seat, she twisted around so I wouldn't have to lean so far.

"Okay," Mama said. "About three months ago, the doctor sent Papa to a heart specialist in the city. They ran a bunch of tests and stuff and—"

I had an awfully hard time getting to sleep. When I finally dozed off, I have no idea. I did remember that the last time I glanced at my clock, it was 12:13.

While we drove to the house, Mama explained that the arteries and veins that came and went to Papa's heart were kind of blocked. "Not bad," Daddy had assured me. "He doesn't have to have surgery, and he's *not* really in any danger. But if he doesn't take care of himself, he will be. They'll have to do bypass surgery or put in a couple of stints. And if they don't . . ."

He kind of stopped and nodded at Mama. I guess she could tell by the look on my face that I didn't know what bypass or stints were, so she explained. It took the rest of the drive. When we stopped in the driveway, I reminded them that Daddy had said: "And if they don't . . ."

Mama opened her door and started unfastening Kate's car seat. Daddy cut the motor off and flung his door opened. I reached out. Put a hand on each of their shoulders.

"And if they don't . . ." I repeated. "What?"

Okay—maybe, sometimes, it's better if us kids *don't* know.

They both assured me that the doctors had caught it early. That Papa was watching his diet, and he and Meme had been walking a mile every day for exercise. And that with everyone keeping a close eye on him, there really wasn't that much to worry about.

But the words, *a possible heart attack,* were the only things that stuck in my head. They kept me awake until after midnight. They haunted my dreams. And when I got up, I felt like I'd spent the whole night fighting with my pillow and the covers, and . . .

The pillow must have won.

chapter 26

When the alarm went off, I punched the snooze button and turned back over. The second time I heard it, it suddenly hit me that we had boxes and the mattress to move, so Mama could sweep under my bed.

I kicked the covers off and sat up. Only I had to stay there a couple of seconds. Not getting enough sleep always made me groggy.

Once I got my balance, I put my robe on and staggered to the kitchen.

Holding Kate, Mama was trying to butter toast and stir the scrambled eggs. Once I sat down, she handed Kate to me so she could finish breakfast. Kate's little eyes sparkled. She cooed and wiggled. Just holding her seemed to relax me. It would be so nice, for just the two of us to sneak into my room and lie down for a little nap. Just a few minutes, and then—

The high-pitched, bloodcurdling scream made me jump. My head snapped around. Eyes closed and face contorted as if in pain, Kate let out another scream.

"Mama . . . ?"

"She had a morning feeding at four thirty," Mama said, calm as always. "She didn't throw up again, did she?"

I glanced at Kate's chin and down at my robe.

"Yes."

Mama scooted the eggs off the burner. Extra diaper in hand, she scurried over to clean up Kate and dab at the streak down the sleeve and side of my robe.

"Is she okay, Mama? What is it? Why does she scream like that?"

Mama took Kate and draped her over one shoulder.

"It's just colic." She smiled. "Anna only had a little touch of it, but when you were a baby, there were times when you would scream bloody murder. I mean, big-time screaming."

I couldn't help notice how the corners of her mouth tugged down from a smile, to a half frown.

"Then again . . . Kate throws up a lot more than you did. I mean . . . well, babies spit up all the time, but Kate . . . she does more than you or Anna put together. I asked Dr. Jenkins about it last time. He thought the same as I did—colic. We're supposed to go in for our regular appointment at eleven this morning. I'll have him check her again.

"Soon as we finish breakfast, we'll stack those boxes and get the mattress off your bed."

I was sleepy and tired. But after Kate screamed in my ear, I was wide awake.

Anna *wasn't* wide awake.

Shaking her and talking to her didn't seem to do one bit of good. So instead of pestering, I just swooped her up in my arms, set her in my lap, and rocked her back and forth. She glared up at me—at first. So to keep her from getting all bent out of shape, I kissed her on the cheek and tickled her. She giggled and kissed me back.

"You ready for breakfast?"

She nodded. When I started to set her down on the bed, she wrapped her arms around my neck. "Carry me," she whined, almost giggling.

"You are a spoiled brat, Miss Anna Lee Rankin. Did you know that?"

"Carry me." She giggled again.

We were almost finished with breakfast by the time Mama got back.

"Is Kate okay?"

Mama nodded. "She's fine." Then she looked at Anna. "Child—I do believe you have more jelly on your chin and nightgown than you got in your mouth. Here." She handed her a napkin. "Wipe your face."

I really had to rush, but we managed to get the boxes out from under my bed, the mattress leaned against the wall, and me dressed in time to make the school bus. I felt pretty good. I'd managed to handle getting Anna up, without a fuss. When I raced out the front door, Mama had Kate up and was nursing her. She wasn't crying. In fact, she acted like she was downright starved.

By the time I got to the bus, plopped down in my seat, and realized how hard I was puffing and panting . . . well . . . I didn't feel so good. It reminded me of Papa. The words *heart attack* jumped into my head and hovered over me like a buzzard all the way to school.

Selena was already in her chair when I got to the room. I walked over to her. Smiled as nice as I could.

"On the math homework, what did you come up with on problem number twenty-four?"

Selena looked up at me. For an instant, she forgot that she was still mad, and smiled. Catching herself, she chased the look from her face and stuck her nose back into her book.

"I haven't done number twenty-four, yet," she mumbled. Then—kind of as an afterthought, she added, "I have to study." She said it real snippylike, too, and never so much as looked up from her book.

I shrugged it off and went to my desk. *Sooner or later,* I thought, *she'll get over it. Maybe.*

First hour we had a pop quiz in social studies. Second hour, I made an A on my math homework, and third hour PE class was an absolute blast. I ate lunch with Carmen and Ellie. The afternoon was kind of dull. We watched films.

We were just getting our stuff together to go home when Mrs. Peck's voice crackled over the intercom.

"Mrs. McMasters? Is Kristine Rankin still there?"

"The bell hasn't rung," she answered, shooting the intercom an irritated glare. "Yes. She's still here."

"Would you tell her she's supposed to ride the bus to her grandparents' today?"

Mrs. McMasters pointed a finger at the intercom and raised her eyebrows. I nodded, so she'd know I got the message.

"I'll tell her, Mrs. Peck. Thank you."

I stuffed my math book into my backpack along with the rest of my stuff. Everything was ready. As soon as the bell rang, I'd dart for the door. I'd go straight out the west end of the building. It was farther to the buses that way, but there usually weren't any kids to dodge around, and it was a lot quicker. I'd get on the bus, kind of fool around near the front until Selena got on. The second she sat down I'd slide in next to her. If she tried to move, I wouldn't let her out. Being trapped next to me on the bus, she'd have to talk. Well . . . at least listen. I'd tell her that I really wasn't trying to avoid her. I would tell her that I wasn't mad at her, and I still wanted her to be my friend. I'd tell her about the dog and the fight with grandpa and . . .

All of a sudden, my head kind of snapped. (I guess it was the fleeting word *grandpa.*) I glanced toward the speaker.

"Mrs. McMasters," I called. "Did she say *which* grandparents' house I was supposed to go to?"

She shook her head. After sitting there for a moment, she sighed, got up, and punched the intercom button. "Mrs. Peck?"

No answer.

"Mrs. Peck?"

Still nothing.

"Either on the intercom to another room or

stuck on the phone." Mrs. McMasters sneered at the speaker. Finally she turned to me. "Got your stuff ready to go home?"

"Yes, ma'am."

She motioned to the door. "Go on down and ask her. Scoot. Before the bell rings."

I darted for the door.

"And don't miss the bus," she called after me.

I can't remember what grade I was in when I figured it out. But the first twenty minutes in the morning, and the last fifteen minutes in the afternoon, were *not* the times to go to the office.

I slung my backpack over my shoulder, crossed the fingers of my left hand, and wished, "Please let today be different. Let me get to the bus early, so I can sit by Selena."

Sometimes you get lucky. Sometimes you don't. Surely I was due for a little good luck.

chapter 27

Sometimes you get lucky. Sometimes you don't. When I opened the door and stepped into the office, I could tell that this was one of those "don't" days.

Mr. Wheat was in his office with his back to the door. Both hands on his hips, he leaned way over, saying something to the two eighth-grade boys who sat in the chairs in front of him. He was getting on to them for something. I didn't recognize either one, though. That's probably because they had their heads hung so low, they almost touched their knees.

Mrs. Peck stood in front of the intercom box. She held the phone against her ear in one hand. "Just a second, and I'll check." She tilted the phone away from her mouth and flipped one of the switches with her free hand. "Mrs. Davidson? Please tell Leslie Smith that her mother will be a little late today.

Make sure she knows she's supposed to wait *inside*. Okay?"

"Okay," a voice crackled back.

The other phone line rang. Mrs. Peck rolled her eyes. "Just a second," she said into the phone. She punched two buttons: "Pioneer Elementary, please hold."

Before she went back to the first person she had on hold, Mrs. Peck turned to me. "Did you get the message, Kristine?"

"Yes, ma'am." I could tell she was really busy, so I added quickly, "Did she say which grand-parents?"

Mrs. Peck stared at her desk. "I've got the note right . . ."

The bell rang. It was a good bell—when we were on the playground—'cause we could hear it no matter how loud we were. Inside—the thing was so noisy, we had to wait until it finished before we could hear a single thing. The second it quit, Mrs. Peck picked up right where she left off. ". . . here on my desk, someplace." She motioned me around the counter. Pointed. "Pink notepaper. Left-hand side."

There was a scrambled pile of about eight or nine pink notepapers on the left side of Mrs. Peck's desk. I scooped them up and tapped them against the flat surface, so I could browse through a neat stack, and not get them out of order. Names were scribbled at the top. Wheat. Wheat. Martin. Arrington. Five notes down I found McMasters.

I scanned the note quickly. The breath caught in my throat. I blinked. Then blinking once more, I read it again. Slow, this time.

Teacher:	McMasters
Student:	Kristine Rankin
Message:	Baby to hospital in city
	Have catch bus to grandparents—W
Time:	1:45

All I could do was stand there and stare at that note. I couldn't blink anymore. I couldn't even breathe. Just stare. Only when the note got so blurry I wasn't able to read it, did I realize my hands and arms were shaking. I let it drop to the table and read it once more.

Mrs. Peck looked over. "Kristine? What's wrong? You getting the flu? You're pale as a ghost."

I pointed down at the pink note. Mrs. Peck raised up on her tiptoes so she could peek over my shoulder.

"Give me a second, Kristine. Let me think."
The phone started ringing again. She ignored it
and stared down at the note. "Okay!" She yelped.
"Now I remember! It's all right, honey! Everything's fine. It's just for some tests. Your mom said
they were just going for a few tests—that's all."
"Are you sure?" Now not just my hands and
arms were shaking. I was trembling all over.
"Positive. Her voice wasn't scared or anything.
She sounded perfectly fine and . . . I'm sure she
said, 'Just tests.'" She wrapped her arm around me
and gave me a big hug. "I'm sorry I scared you. I
don't take very good notes. Jot 'em short and
quick, especially when we're busy. Are you okay?"
The air whooshed out of me so hard, I felt my
bangs bounce.
"Yes, ma'am. I'm fine."
All the time she stared at the note thinking, and
all the time she was talking to me, the phone just
kept ringing.
"Oh, Kristine." Mrs. Peck gave me another
little squeeze. "Did you figure out which house
you're supposed to go to?"
I glanced at the note one more time, just to
make sure.
"Grandma and Grandpa Wilson's." I smiled,
when I saw the letter "W" after "grandparents."

Then realizing how quiet the halls were, I spun around and raced for the bus. "Thank you for helping me, Mrs. Peck," I yelled.

Mrs. Martin had just closed the door and started the bus rolling, when I came tearing up the sidewalk.

"Sorry," I gasped, taking the steps two at a time. "I was in the office."

She nodded and jabbed a thumb toward the back. "No problem. Going to your grandmother Wilson's today, huh? Go find a seat." As I turned and started walking toward the back of the bus, I could hear her add, "Shouldn't be any problem. Everybody's going home with the flu. There are quite a few empty . . ."

I didn't hear the rest of it. Kimmie Sales was in the seat next to Selena. When Selena saw me coming up the aisle, she turned her head to look out the window. I slid into the first empty seat I came to. There were two first graders across the aisle from me, and two third-grade girls in the seat behind me. I didn't notice who was behind them—not at first, anyway.

"What's Curley Sue doing on our bus? She hasn't ridden with us for a couple of months."

"Yeah, and she's late, too," another voice chimed in.

"You guys better not be callin' her 'Curley Sue.' She really gets ticked off about it." I recognized Matt Green's voice. "Last time I called her that, she almost took my head off with a dodge ball."

I didn't even bother to look around. I'd been so scared. No, not scared. Terrified. But after Mrs. Peck talked to me and assured me that it was just for tests, and there was nothing wrong . . . I felt so much better that nothing else mattered. Selena could be a total snot. The boys could pester all they wanted. I didn't care.

I took a deep breath and slid down in the seat. Kind of snuggled into it and closed my eyes so I could relax.

Only trouble, when I closed my eyes, those words seemed to burn on the insides of my eyelids: **Baby to hospital in city.**

My eyes sprang wide. When I was little, I used to look at the sun. Mama, Daddy, Meme C—everybody—told me not to stare at the sun. Sometimes I did it, anyway. When I closed my eyes, the sun was still there, like it was burning on the insides of my eyelids.

When I got a little older, I quit doing dumb stuff like that. But, sometimes, on a bright day, I would look at the black wrought-iron posts on our front porch. When I closed my eyes, they were still there. Only instead of being black, they were almost white against the darkness inside my eyelids. That's the way **Baby to hospital in city** looked—almost burning white against the dark.

But why would they have to take her to the hospital? Maybe it was 'cause she screamed when her tummy hurt. Maybe she threw up too much. Maybe it wasn't colic at all. Maybe it was something *real* serious. Maybe it was . . .

Kristine, shut up! I screamed inside my head. *Quit being so scared. There's nothing to be scared about. Meme C will tell you everything when you get to her house. Just relax. Quit trying to worry yourself and calm down.*

And that's just what I did—until I got to Meme C's house. Up until then, I had no idea what *scared* really was.

chapter 28

I was in such a hurry to find Meme, and make sure Kate was *really* okay, I didn't even glance at my "thinking log" when I ran up the drive. There wasn't one single thought about Dandy. Eyes on the house, I slowed to a jog about halfway up the hill. Still a little worried, I was walking by the time I got to the front porch.

You're gonna have to start getting in shape for softball, I told myself. *Hard as you're breathing, you won't even be able to make it around the bases.*

The front screen was closed, but the thick wooden door behind it was open. Meme C always left the door opened when she was expecting me.

"I'm here, Meme," I called, tossing my backpack on the chair beside the front door. "What's wrong with Kate? Why did they have to take her to the city for tests? Is it serious, or . . .

"Meme?"

Must be in the kitchen. Got the dishwasher going, or putting something in the stove and can't hear me.

"Meme?"

The kitchen was empty. There was a bowl of cookie dough sitting beside the oven. The oven wasn't on, but it looked like the dough had been dug into. When I dipped my finger in for a quick taste, I noticed the top was a little crusty—like it had been sitting for a while. I frowned.

Why would Meme leave cookie dough out?

I don't know what made me peek inside the oven, but when I did, there was a cookie sheet filled with half-baked cookies. They were still smushy and hadn't even flattened out yet. Cautiously I touched the cookie sheet. It was warm but not hot. The oven had been off for a while.

That's weird. Must be cleaning out a closet or something.

I checked the bedrooms. No one.

I was practically running by the time I finished searching through the whole house. There was no one home. Not a single soul. No note. Nothing!

Maybe I read Mrs. Peck's note wrong. Maybe it was grandparents—R, instead of grandparents with a W after it.

I shook my head. *No! I know Mrs. Peck had it*

written: grandparents—W. I darted to the kitchen, practically ripped the phone off the holder, and dialed Grandma and Grandpa Rankin's number.

There was no answer. Thinking maybe I'd dialed the wrong number, I hung up and dialed again.

A lot of things can go through your head while you're waiting for someone to pick up a phone.

First thing you have to do is calm down, I told myself. *They're here someplace. Don't act like a little kid and panic. Just relax.*

But it simply didn't make sense. The front door was open. When Mama was at work, I always rode the bus over here. There were a few times—not many, but a few—when they would have to go someplace. They always locked the front door and left a note on the screen. Right where I would be sure to see it. Meme had shown me the fake rock at the edge of the garden. The key was inside.

Cookies were started in the oven, then turned off. Dough—which Meme always kept in the fridge, or at least covered with a towel—was left to dry beside the stove. There was nobody home! They wouldn't do stuff like that if they were going someplace.

Maybe the barn.

I don't know how many times the phone rang. I

quit counting on seven, hung the stupid thing up, and raced outside.

Papa's barn was humongous. In the old days, when I was little, he used to store small bales of hay in the west end of it. Now that he had the round baler, he kept it there, along with his tractor and other farm machinery. On the southeast side of the barn was a big workroom. There were all sorts of tools and stuff in it. Right next to that was a place to put the truck inside when the weather was really bad.

The first thing I noticed, when I got outside, was that the truck wasn't in the driveway. I hadn't even looked as I walked up the drive, because I knew they were home. *That's probably what it is,* I thought. *Papa had trouble with the old truck and has it up in the barn next to the workroom. He just needed Meme to help him with something.*

The workroom was dark as pitch. "Meme? Papa? Where are you? What's going on?"

No answer.

I raced around to the other end of the barn. "Papa?" I called. "Where have you been? I've hunted all over for you and Meme, and . . . and . . ."

No one was in the barn. The baler and other farm stuff was there, but no tractor. And NO PAPA!

"Where are you?" I whined. Only, it wasn't really a whine. It was more like a scream.

I felt the shaking start again—just like when I read the note at school about baby Kate. I wanted to scream as loud as I could, so they would hear me. I wanted to run. Run and find them. I wanted to . . .

Instead, I forced myself to relax. I took three really deep breaths. The smell of alfalfa and barn dust tickled my nose. I clenched my fists to keep my hands from trembling. Took another deep breath and held it.

That's when I heard the sound. An engine. A smile tugged the corners of my mouth.

It was Papa's tractor.

Almost laughing, I practically skipped outside. Following the sound, I reached the corner and stopped. There. There's the tractor. It was about fifty yards out in the pasture. A round bale of hay was still on the spear at the back. The cows were clumped around, nudging and shoving one another, to fight their way up and get a mouthful of hay from the bale. Papa wasn't sitting on the tractor, and with all the cows around . . .

My heart sank.

What if Papa had fallen off the tractor? What if he'd had a heart attack and the cows had trampled him? What if—

Waving my arms and screaming at the top of my lungs, I raced to the tractor and charged into the herd. Shoving and butting to get the others out of their way, the cows dodged aside.

It was such a relief to find that Papa wasn't there! It was just the cows, trying to get some hay.

My feeling of relief didn't even last the length of time it took me to blink. *Why would Papa leave the tractor running? Why would he leave the twine? He was always worried that his cows might swallow some of it. Where were Meme C and Papa?*

I hopped up on the tractor and turned off the ignition key. I climbed up and stood on the seat, scanning the pasture.

No one in the field. No one at the edge of the trees to my left. Nothing. Just me and the cows.

I jumped down and ran to the house.

No one answered at Grandma and Grandpa Rankin's. No one answered at the school. I glanced at the clock. It was 4:45. They'd already gone home. So I called Selena.

I didn't want to. She hadn't been very nice lately. But then again, I had lied to her about studying and . . . and . . .

And . . . Selena was the only friend I had. I needed help!

Maybe her mom could come over and tell me what to do. Maybe she knew something about Meme and Papa, and why they weren't here.

Maybe Selena's dad could tell us something. He worked at a hospital in the city. Maybe they could reach him on the phone, and he could call around and find where Mama and Kate were. Maybe he could tell us how really bad Kate was.

Maybe it was serious. Maybe it was more than serious.

If baby Kate was so sick she might die . . .

What other reason was there for Meme and Papa to go off and leave the house? They knew I was coming. Why else would Papa leave the tractor running or Meme leave her cookie dough out on the counter?

It had to be a *real* emergency. Something so serious and scary that everyone dropped what they were doing, forgot about me, and . . . and . . .

No answer at the Rankins'. No answer at school. Selena's number rang and rang and rang and . . .

The phone felt so heavy I could hardly hang it up. I stood there a moment, then walked to the front door. Mattie barked as I jogged past the back fence. She bounded along beside me, yapping and leaping against the chain link. I trotted past the barn, beneath the tin roof where I threw the softball to practice catching. And, once past the barn . . .

I ran.

I ran and ran and ran—as if . . . if I could run fast enough and far enough and hard enough—I could leave the scared feeling behind. I could escape the fear that gnawed at my stomach. Elude the panic that forced the pounding of my heart so high in my throat, I felt like I was going to choke. Get away from the horrible premonition that my baby sister was dying, or my grandfather had had a heart attack, or—

Both.

chapter 29

Mama and Daddy always said, "You can't run away from your problems."

Meme and Papa said the same thing. Shoot! Practically everybody said it.

They were all wrong.

When I finally stopped running, I was near the pond, way at the far south end of the farm. All the feelings that had been tangled up inside of me were gone. There was no fear. No perception of being deserted and totally alone. No panic or thoughts about all the *bad things* that must have happened.

That's because I didn't have time to think.

I was too busy trying to breathe.

So weak and tired I could barely lift them anymore, my legs stopped before the rest of me was ready. They simply didn't work anymore. Trembly and wobbly as warm Jell-O, I felt like I was going to fall over. So I sank to my knees and rocked back to sit on my heels. I put my hands on the ground to keep from tipping over sideways. My whole body heaved up and down, straining desperately for air.

How long I sat there, rocking back and forth on my heels, I don't know. When I finally got where I could breathe without gasping, I felt like I was going to be sick.

Slowly I lay down on my side. Knees tucked and arms folded over my tummy, I stared at the grass. Concentrated on slowing my breathing.

Okay, so maybe all those people who told me "You can't run away from your problems" weren't wrong after all. I outran my problems for a few minutes.

Lying there, staring at the grass and dirt, my breathing came easier, more relaxed. And as soon as that happened, the worry started creeping back into my head again. I realized I hadn't run away from them. As soon as I slowed down, they just caught up with me once more.

Maybe Papa was already gone. *I never got to tell him how much—how really, really much—I loved him. Never told him what a truly wonderful grandpa he was. How much fun. What if I never got to? What if I never got to thank him for taking me fishing or playing catch with me? What if I could never . . .*

ever . . . again . . . have him spin me around the kitchen floor while he sang that silly song. What if there were no more of his dumb jokes to laugh at, or no more playing like I was irritated when he called me Squirt or . . .

Eyes closed, the tears felt warm as they rolled down my cheeks.

What if I could never play dolls with baby Kate? Or play dress up?

"It's not fair!" I raged.

"It's not right!"

Kate needs time to grow up. She needs time to have a best friend. Even one who gets mad at her sometimes. She's so little and helpless. She needs the chance to go to school. She needs to have someone to talk with about clothes and shoes and boys and . . . and . . .

The touch was so soft at first, I hardly noticed. Gentle as a butterfly's wing touching the petal of a flower, it brushed my cheek.

. . . and she needs a kitten of her very own. One she can play with and giggle at when it chases the string across her bed. She needs a horse. She needs to feel the wind . . .

The touch came again. I opened my eyes.

Mattie lay beside me. She wasn't leaping around and wiggling all over, like she usually did.

She just lay there, watching me. Her big brown eyes seemed worried. Her tongue kissed away another tear.

. . . to feel the wind blow through her hair as she gallops across the pasture. Kate needs to grow up and have a horse and a grandpa . . . and . . .

Crawling on her tummy, Mattie eased closer. When I put my hand across her back, she licked it. Gently. Tenderly. She was worried about me. Sad because I was sad. She was careful with me, because she could tell how much I hurt. And all she wanted to do was help.

. . . and Kate needed to have a puppy to hold and play with and . . . and . . . love.

I swooped Mattie up in my arm and hugged her close against me. She nestled her head on my chest and lay perfectly still. I loved her and held her. She looked at me with those big brown worried eyes and whined. A soft little sound as if asking, "Are you all right?" And as if to say, "I love you."

"I love you, too," I said back.

And I really did.

She loved me. That was all that mattered to her. And the only thing I could do was—

Love her back.

Just because.

* * *

I raised up on one elbow. With the other hand, I held her close to my heart. "It's gonna be okay," I told her. "No matter what happens or how bad it is, it's gonna be okay."

Staring down my chin at her, I felt my eyebrows dip. The corners of my mouth tugged down. My head tilted to one side.

"What are you doing here, anyway, you little scamp? How did you get out of the pen?"

Wagging her tail, she licked me on the chin.

"There you are!"

The sound of a voice made me jerk.

"I knew that pup would find you. But she took off . . . so fast . . . I thought I'd lost her."

Matt Green stood a few feet away. Bent over with his hands on his knees, his sides heaved in and out. Even as far away as he was I could hear him huffing and puffing.

"That pup must be . . . part bloodhound," he panted. "Stuck her nose . . . to the ground . . . and . . ." He could only talk between breaths. ". . . took off like a shot. Ran straight to you." He puffed a little more, then straightened and walked toward us.

"Are you okay? You got a twisted ankle? Your leg broke?"

"I'm okay," I answered. "Why?"

"Well, you're lying there on the ground, and . . ."

"I'm just resting. Are *you* okay?"

"Me?"

"Yeah, you. You're panting like . . . like . . . and what are you doing here, anyway? And how did Mattie get here? Did you let her out of the backyard? Why would you do something like that? What if she'd gotten out in the road and a car had come along? And . . ."

Matt leaned down and held a finger up—right between my eyes.

"Hold it! One question at a time." He straightened and took a deep breath. "I'm panting because, for a little pup, that dog's the fastest thing I ever saw in my life. I nearly lost her twice." He held up two fingers. "Mattie's here because I let her out of the yard." Now three fingers. "The reason I did something like that is to find you."

"Me?"

"Yes, you! Your grandpa's got half the country out looking for you. Where have you been, anyway?"

"My grandpa? Papa Wilson? He's alive? You've seen him? Is he all right?"

Matt kind of curled his lip and gave me a funny look.

"No, he's not all right. He's worried half sick because nobody could find you."

"I was at the house. *They* weren't there!"

"You weren't at the house when they called. You didn't answer when Mrs. Peck called. When Mama, Daddy, and I got there, we couldn't find you, either. We didn't know if somebody kidnapped you, or you were walking back to school, or . . . or—

"Well, Mattie was the only one who had the slightest idea where you were. She kept jumping against the back corner of the fence. Where she was looking and the way she was acting, I finally figured you were in the barn. But when I couldn't find you—" He jammed his fists against his hips and glared down at me. "Look. We need to get you home. We got a bunch of people scared and worried. A bunch runnin' all over the country lookin' for you. Come on."

Holding Mattie against me with one arm, I used the other to help turn and get to my knees. It wasn't until I tried to stand up that I figured out I'd run *way* too far, and then sat *way* too long!

Both legs cramped up. The calf muscle in my left leg wadded into a knot about the size of a softball. The big muscle, above the knee and on the front of my right leg, tightened like a rubber band, right before you shoot it across the room. My eyes flashed as I plopped back to my seat and frantically started rubbing my thigh.

"What's wrong? Leg cramps?"

I nodded, and tried to say yes, but the only thing that came out was a little squeak.

Matt dropped to one knee and reached out to help me rub it. Just as he was about to touch my leg, he yanked his hands back like he'd grabbed hold of a hot cookie sheet.

"It's a leg," I said between gritted teeth. "Not a rattlesnake."

"I—ah—er—" he stammered. Clearing his throat, he stood up and held out a hand. "You need to get on your feet. Stretch it out, instead of . . . ah . . . rubbing it. Here, I'll hold Mattie."

"No, I'll hold Mattie," I said. I couldn't help notice how red his cheeks were. I reached out a hand. "Just help me up."

Boys are so weird sometimes.

There was a part of me that wanted to tease him. Give him a hard time about being afraid to touch a "girl" leg. A part of me wanted to say something like, "What's wrong? Afraid you're gonna get cooties?" and maybe laugh at him.

But there was another part that just wanted to hug him around the neck, and thank him for finding me. Thank him from the bottom of my heart for telling me that Papa was okay, and they were home, and . . .

Well, I let him help me up.

chapter 30

The muscle cramps eased, not long after I got to my feet. I stood for a couple of minutes, took a few steps, and they were mostly gone. My legs still ached, but they didn't hurt. I could walk just fine.

I didn't let Matt know that.

He held on to my left hand while I hobbled and limped around for a minute or two. Then, not knowing what else to do, he put my left arm around his neck. Held onto my wrist where it draped over his shoulder.

At first, he didn't know what to do with his right hand. He started to hold on to my waist, then my hip, then quickly to my elbow, then my arm. The way his hand kept moving around—hunting the right place to get hold—well, I had to clamp my lips together to keep from giggling at him.

Mattie didn't wiggle or struggle. She just lay

quietly in the bend of my right arm, watching Matt. Almost glaring at him whenever I moaned or flinched, as if she'd tear him up if he hurt me. Finally, Matt just got hold around my waist. Sort of like helping an injured football player off the field, he walked beside me, holding me up.

It felt kind of good.

I guess Mattie could tell, because when I glanced down she almost seemed to smile up at me. Her tail thumped against my side.

At the barn I told him I was okay and could walk by myself. He took my arm from around his shoulder, but still held my hand—just to support me if I happened to fall.

That felt kind of good, too.

Papa's pickup was in the drive, where it belonged. A big, yellow school bus was behind it, beside a white car and Selena's van.

Papa stood on the porch. Hand cupped at the bill of his cap, he scanned one direction then the other. When he spotted us, he yanked the cap from his head and waved it back and forth. Mr. Wheat pulled into the drive. Papa didn't even stop to say hi. He pointed up the hill, where Matt and I were, gave the okay sign, and jogged toward us. Mr. Wheat got out and went inside.

Papa looked fine. He wasn't pale. He wasn't holding his chest. He wasn't even breathing hard when he reached out to hug me. But when he wrapped his arms around me, his big hands shook so hard they felt like vibrators on my back.

"Are you okay, Kristine? Are you hurt? What happened? When we couldn't find you . . . we . . . we . . ." His voice was quivering so much he couldn't talk. ". . . we were so scared."

"I'm fine, Papa." I couldn't keep my own voice from quivering. "When I couldn't find you and Meme, I got scared, too, . . . and . . . and—"

"Where were you?" he demanded.

"Mattie found her up by the pond," Matt answered, when I couldn't.

"The pond? What were you doing, there?"

"She was trying to find you and Mrs. Wilson," Matt spoke up quickly. I think he really knew there was more to it than just looking for them. But that's all he said.

I hugged Papa as hard as I could, then kind of leaned to the side so I could peek around him. "Why are all these cars and the bus here? Is something wrong with Kate? Where's Mama and Daddy? Kate's not sick, is she? They didn't have a wreck or something, did they?"

Papa held my shoulders and scooted me square in front of him.

"Everyone's fine, Kristine! I swear!"

"But why are all these cars here? And where were you and Meme?"

"Your grandmother," he began. His voice was real funny. Kind of irritated—yet relieved—both at the same time. But he didn't finish what he started to say. Instead he just put a hand on my shoulder and moved me toward the house. "It'd be best if you just came inside and saw for yourself." He smiled. "She's fine, but . . . we'll let her tell you what she did. As for why all the cars are here . . ."

On the way to the house, Papa told me that he tried to call. The first time was probably while I was still on the bus or coming up the hill. He waited about fifteen to twenty minutes (long enough for me to head for the barn), then dialed a second time. When he still couldn't get me, he called the school. Mrs. Peck called Selena, to see if I had gone home with her, instead of to Meme C's, then she called Grandma and Grandpa Rankin, then some of my other friends. Mr. Wheat and the custodian heard her. The principal drove out to find the bus, and the custodian started walking, to see if I was headed back to school. While all that was going on, Papa called Matt's mom and dad, since their house was closest, to see if they'd come over and find me. The thing kind of snowballed. It wasn't what you'd call an "official search party," but there were a whole bunch of people either walking cross country or driving around in their cars, looking for me.

As we walked past the back gate, Matt offered to take Mattie, but I wanted to hold onto her just a little longer. Holding her kind of soothed me. I think being in my arms made Mattie feel a little safer, too. She wasn't used to seeing all these cars in her yard.

"Catherine," Papa called when he opened the front door. "Tell Kristine what you did to—"

The words stopped when Papa saw she wasn't in the living room. A frown wrinkled his furrowed brow.

"Catherine Louise Wilson!" His voice boomed so loud it seemed to rattle the walls. "Where are you?"

Meme peeked around the kitchen doorway.

"I was on the phone. Marie was on her cell phone letting people know Kristine is okay. The kitchen phone started ringing. I just got up for a minute."

Papa's eyes narrowed. He jabbed an angry finger at the rocking chair. Meme put a finger to her lips, shushing him before he even has a chance to say anything.

"That was Lauren," she explained. "They stopped for gas and should be home in about thirty minutes."

"Is Kate okay?"

"She's fine. The doctors ran some tests and said there was nothing serious. Said she'd probably outgrow it."

"What is it, Meme? What's she got?"

Meme held out her hand, showing me where she'd written on her palm with an ink pen.

"It's called gastroesophageal reflux."

"What's that?"

"I think that's the highfalutin' doctor's name for colic. She's safe. She's okay."

Papa walked between us and gently nudged me aside. "Old woman!" he scolded. "You're always chewing on me for not minding the doctor. What did *your* doctor tell you to do?"

"Oh, all right." Meme let Papa lead her to the chair. She plopped down in her rocker and gave him kind of a smart-aleck smile. "Happy now?"

"You're supposed to stay there and be still for the next couple of hours. Remember? Show Kristine what you did."

Meme crinkled her nose at him. "It wasn't all my fault. I told you to leave a note on the front door." She motioned me over to sit on the arm of the couch next to her chair. "Old coot was in such a panic, he wouldn't even listen to me," she whispered.

Once I was sitting beside her, Meme rocked forward. Ducking her head, she reached up and parted her hair with the tips of her fingers. I frowned, looking at the bald spot she showed me. It was a neat rectangle—about an inch or two long and a half inch to an inch wide. Right in the middle was a little line laced together with stitches.

"What happened, Meme?"

"Oh," she sighed. "I was trying to get a wooden box down from the top of the closet. Darned thing slipped and clunked me right on the noggin."

"Did it hurt?"

"Yeah, it hurt. I went to the kitchen to get an ice pack and check the cookies. That's when I noticed the blood."

"Was there a lot?"

"Was there a lot!" Papa yelped. "Never saw so much blood. It was shooting out. Looked like that geyser up in Wyoming—you know, Old Faithful."

Meme ignored him and smiled at me. "Any time

you get even a small scratch on your head, it's gonna bleed a little."

"A little?" Papa scoffed. "How about your blouse, the four dishtowels you soaked, the seat of the truck and—"

"Larry. Quit exaggerating! You're gonna scare the poor child half to death."

Meme winked at me. "Old windbag's just full of hot air. There was a little blood, but—"

"Hi, Kristine," Mrs. Peck said, peeking around the corner from the kitchen. "Glad you're okay." She turned to Meme C. "Catherine, I've called all of the people who have cell phones to let them know Kristine is home and safe. Mr. Wheat and Mrs. Martin are going to take the bus and see if they can find some of the others. The ones they miss will probably come by the house. I'll go stand out in the yard so they won't come traipsing through and bother you."

Hands on the arms of her rocker, Meme tilted forward and lifted herself out of the chair. Papa almost shoved me off the arm of the couch and pushed Matt aside, when he darted between us to stand directly in front of her.

"Just where do you think you're going?"

Meme nodded toward the kitchen. "Got all these folks coming. Some of 'em been walkin' all over the country, hunting your granddaughter. Least we could do is show a little hospitality. I need to fix a fresh batch of cookies to feed them. There's pop, chips, and nuts in the pantry. I'll—"

"You'll sit right there in that chair, like the doctor told you!" Papa cut her off. "I can fix the drinks and—"

"I'll help with the chips and nuts," Mrs. Peck offered.

"I'll fix the cookies," I chimed in.

Reluctantly, Meme sank back down in her rocking chair.

"I'll help her." Matt smiled.

Mouth flopped open, my head whipped around.

"What?" he smiled. "You don't think guys can make cookies?"

I started to say something, but Meme C gave a quick tug on my pant leg. "Careful, Kristine," she whispered. "That young man's been helping bake cookies since he was five. His grandmother is the one I got my cookie recipe from."

chapter 31

Meme took Mattie. I was a bit reluctant to hand her over because I thought she might wiggle and try to climb up to kiss her. Mattie must have sensed that we were worried about Meme. She simply curled up in her lap, licked the back of her arm a moment, then went to sleep. "Be sure and wash your hands before you start on the cookies," Meme whispered.

I nodded.

Papa started pulling drinks, chips, and nuts from the pantry, while Mrs. Peck prowled through the cabinets to find nice bowls to put them in.

While I dumped the old crusty cookie dough, Matt washed the cookie sheet and pre-heated the oven. I knew where Meme kept the sugar, flour, and measuring cups. I got those while Matt found the eggs and butter in the fridge.

When it came to mixing, Matt took over. He didn't even use the recipe. He added a full cup of brown sugar, instead of three-quarters of a cup, three lids full of vanilla instead of one, and half the baking soda that the recipe on the chocolate chip package called for.

"Makes 'em chewier," he informed me.

Then we stirred and stirred and stirred. It went pretty quick and easy until we started adding the flour. Matt had me hold the mixing bowl so he could use both hands on the wooden spoon. A little bigger and stronger than I was, he ended up dragging and jerking me, and the mixing bowl, all over the top of the counter. We had flour everywhere—even on us. So he latched onto the bowl and told me to stir. That was just as bad.

It was fun, though. We laughed and giggled and slopped flour all over the place. Matt even wiped some off the cabinet with his hand, then smeared it on my cheek. I got him back.

By the time people started arriving, we were taking the first batch of cookies off the sheet. Papa had me help Mrs. Peck take drink orders while he put ice in the glasses. Everyone seemed happy to see me. I didn't even have to tell them the whole story about how we'd missed each other. Meme did that while I ran back and forth to the kitchen.

I *did* have to tell Mama and Daddy. When they got home to find all the cars and the people, they almost flipped out.

Grandma and Grandpa Rankin came next. Both rushed to the kitchen to give me a big hug and tell me how scared they had been. Meme let Anna take Mattie outside. Anna giggled and laughed and chased Mattie all over the backyard. Mattie wagged her tail and chased Anna right back. Since Mattie and Anna were outside playing, Meme C took Kate so Mama could help us serve our company.

Curled up on Meme's lap, Kate slept through the whole thing.

It's amazing how babies can do that. I mean, with all the people coming and going, all the talking, all the noise and moving around, and . . . well, it's just down-right amazing.

After I made sure everyone had something to drink, I filled the nut bowl again, then went outside to play with Anna and Mattie. It wasn't long before Matt joined us. We ran and chased and talked and laughed. It was almost dark when we went inside. All of us, including Mattie, were pretty much worn out.

My family and Matt's mom and dad were the only ones left. Kate was awake. Meme C rocked her and talked to her. When I put Mattie down, she raced to Meme and put her paws on her knees. When she saw Kate there, she wagged her tail, gave her a little kiss on the leg, then curled up at Meme's feet.

"Catherine," Mrs. Green said. "Think we've got your kitchen in pretty good shape. Lauren swept the living room, the rest of us polished off the last of the cookies and washed the dishes. Since we're not sure where the serving bowls belong, you think Larry can take care of putting things back in the cabinets?"

"I'm fine," Meme smiled. "I'm tired of sitting in this old rocking chair, anyway. I'll just—"

"You'll just stay put!" Papa glared down at her. "I'm capable of putting things away."

Meme rolled her eyes. "He'll put it away," she whispered, loud enough for all of us to hear. "But it'll take me months to find it again."

Papa stuck his tongue out at her and walked Matt and his folks to the door. Grandma and Grandpa Rankin left a few minutes after they did. We stayed and visited a while longer.

When we were ready to leave, Papa finally let Meme C out of her chair so she could come and see us off.

Daddy carried Anna. Mama held Kate. I snuggled Mattie. I could feel her tail whacking against my back and she kept trying to lean out and lick Meme C and Papa. Of course, she was trying to kiss Mama and Daddy and Anna, too. And they were going with us.

"I'm totally pooped." Daddy kissed Meme on the cheek. "Working this morning, spending the afternoon at the doctor's, and all the excitement around here when we got home . . . I'm ready to go to bed."

He gave Anna a little toss and hugged her when she giggled. Mama cuddled Kate in her arms. Meme and Papa kissed them both, then followed us to the porch. At the doorway, Mattie and I kissed Papa and Meme C good-by. "I hope your head feels better," I told her.

Meme touched the top of her head. "It already does. I'm fine."

I smiled up at Papa. "How are you feeling?"

He glanced down where Mattie lay, curled in the crook of my arm, gently gnawing my thumb with her sharp little puppy teeth. Then he smiled back at me. "I'm doin' good. How about you?"

Mattie nestled her head against my chest. I winked at Papa. "We couldn't be better."